P9-DWS-818

PLAYING FOR THE COMMANDANT

PLAYING
FOR THE
COMMANDANT

Suzy Zail

CANDLEWICK PRESS

For the children sent to the left

The epigraph on page v is from *Long Walk to Freedom* by Nelson Mandela and is reproduced with the kind permission from his publishers, Little, Brown and Company.

The author and publisher thank Dr. Bill Anderson, Honorary Senior Research Fellow at the University of Melbourne and consultant historian and lecturer at the Jewish Holocaust Museum and Research Centre, for his generosity and expertise in reading this book.

This is a work of fiction. Names, characters, places, and incidents are either products of the author's imagination or, if real, are used fictitiously.

Copyright © 2012 by Suzy Zail

All rights reserved. No part of this book may be reproduced, transmitted, or stored in an information retrieval system in any form or by any means, graphic, electronic, or mechanical, including photocopying, taping, and recording, without prior written permission from the publisher.

First U.S. edition 2014

Library of Congress Catalog Card Number 2013955694
ISBN 978-0-7636-6403-9

14 15 16 17 18 19 BVG 10 9 8 7 6 5 4 3 2 1

Printed in Berryville, VA, U.S.A.

This book was typeset in Garamond.

Candlewick Press
99 Dover Street
Somerville, Massachusetts 02144

visit us at www.candlewick.com

No one is born hating another person because of the color of his skin, or his background, or his religion. People must learn to hate, and if they can learn to hate, they can be taught to love, for love comes more naturally to the human heart than its opposite.

NELSON MANDELA

Chapter 1

They came at midnight, splintering the silence with their fists, pounding at our door until Father let them in. I tiptoed to my sister's bed, threw back the covers, and slid in beside her. She was already awake.

"I hate them," I whispered. Mother didn't like us using the word *hate*, but there was no getting around it; I hated them. I hated their perfectly pressed uniforms and the way they pushed past Father, dragging the mud from their boots across Mother's Persian rug. I hated them for nailing the synagogue doors shut and for burning our books. But mostly I hated them for how they made me feel: scared and small.

Erika pressed a finger to her lips. They were in the next room. I crept out of bed and peered into the living room. There were two of them: one was short, the other tall. Both were ugly. I hadn't seen them in the ghetto before, but there had been others with the same helmets and heavy black boots. The last pair who'd visited came for the radio. *Jews aren't allowed to have radios,* they'd said, wrenching the cord from the wall.

My father lit a candle. Mother stood behind him in slippered feet, her hair still in pins. The smaller of the two officers—a young man with a pockmarked face—was rifling through drawers, plucking silver spoons and napkin rings from their velvet sleeves and slipping them into his pocket. I couldn't hear what the taller officer was saying, but after he finished talking, Father reached into the pocket of his dressing gown and pulled out the keys to our apartment.

The officer took the keys. He drew two sheets of paper from his satchel, thrust one at Father, and read the other out loud.

"By order of the Royal Hungarian Government, made this day, Tuesday the twentieth day of June, 1944, all persons of Jewish descent . . ."

We were to assemble outside the synagogue at eight o'clock the following morning. We were allowed one bag each and enough food for three days.

"You're being resettled," the officer said. "We're closing the ghetto."

He didn't say where we were going or how we would get there. He read the brutal words without pausing for breath, then he pulled another sheet from his bag and shone his flashlight on it.

"Samuel Mendel," he said, looking down at my father. "According to this list, you have two daughters. Get them."

Erika didn't wait for Father to call her. She stepped out of the shadows and stood in the doorway in her bare feet, her flimsy nightdress caught in the glare of the flashlight.

"Erika Mendel?" The officer aimed his beam through her thin cotton gown. His face was cold, his eyes hard. My sister nodded.

"Hanna Mendel?"

I stepped into the hallway. The officer shoved me aside and stepped into the bedroom. I watched him fling open cupboards and empty the drawers. It didn't make any sense. They couldn't be kicking us out of the ghetto. It was their idea to create it, their idea to cram us inside its claustrophobic walls. We'd done everything they'd asked of us. We'd painted yellow stars on our apartment buildings, we'd obeyed curfew, we didn't take buses or use the telephone. I wasn't a troublemaker. I was a straight-A student. I'd won a scholarship to the Budapest Conservatorium of Music. I was smart. I was talented.

Erika had told me that none of that mattered, but I'd refused to listen. *When they look at you, they don't see a girl who hands her homework in on time,* she'd said. *They don't care that you wake at six every morning to practice piano. They don't see a concert pianist when they look at you — they see a Jew.*

The officer crouched down on one knee and looked under my bed. I pressed my mouth to my sister's ear.

"Where are we going?"

Erika looked at our father's face, etched with fear, and at our mother, standing next to him, wringing her hands.

"I don't know," she whispered, "but anywhere has to be better than here."

We'd been living in the ghetto for six weeks. It had only taken a few days for the walls to go up around us, hemming us in. Erika hated the ghetto. She hated curfew, and the guards at the gates. She hated that her friends couldn't visit her, or telephone, once the line was disconnected. She missed going to the cinema and eating Sacher torte at Café Gerbeaud. She missed the admiring glances of young men and the way they fought for her attention. One by one, they had all donned uniforms and stopped talking to her. She hated Hitler.

I just thought he was crazy. Before our radio was confiscated, I'd heard him rant about Jews on the BBC. We were a threat to the nation, he said. We stole people's jobs, we ate too much, and we spread disease. I didn't think anyone in Hungary would take him seriously—but then the German tanks rolled into Budapest in March 1944, and the government started passing these crazy laws. Father's business was shut down and his bank account was frozen. We couldn't ride in trains or go to university.

Having blue eyes and blond hair, I didn't attract the attention of the black-booted SS soldiers who patrolled the streets. Not until April, when, in keeping with the führer's orders, Mother sewed a yellow star on all of my clothes—a six-pointed Star of David as big as my palm, inscribed with the German word for Jew: *Jude.*

I wished I could wear my star proudly, as Erika did. We weren't a strictly religious family, but the way Erika saw it, if she had to be stamped a Jew, she'd make her own labels. She found a length of bright-yellow silk at Zimmerman's haberdashery on Utvar Street and fashioned her own glimmering stars that she wore proudly on her left breast. I hid mine when I could, under scarves, my hair, my schoolbag strap.

There were others at school branded like me, and it made me feel a little less alone. But I hated that star. It changed everything. The girls I spent every lunchtime with told me that they would understand if I felt more comfortable eating with my Jewish classmates. My best friend stopped inviting me over.

At least I still had Bach and Beethoven for company.

The officers had moved into our living room. The young one with the bulging pockets was seated at the piano, running his sweaty fingers over the keys. He hit middle C.

"Nice piano. An August Förster," he said, turning to look at his colleague. "I've always wanted an August Förster."

"Take it," the older officer said. "Come back for it tomorrow with the truck."

Erika pulled away from me. "Don't!" I pleaded. I grabbed her arm and held it tight. "Don't go in there. You'll get us in trouble. He won't let us keep it, and even if he did," I whispered, "I can't take it with me."

Erika froze at the sound of our mother's voice.

"Please, sir." My mother stepped toward the officer, tears streaking her face. "Not the piano—"

"Shut up!" The older officer swung his flashlight at my mother, and she leaped back in fright.

He turned to my father. "The synagogue. Tomorrow. Eight o'clock." He opened the front door and stepped into the corridor. The young officer smiled and followed him out.

"They can't do this. We won't let them." Erika ran to the piano.

Father locked the front door. "We need to start packing. We have a lot to do." He took my sister by the shoulders and steered her back to the bedroom. My mother sat slumped at the piano, her head bowed. I sat beside her.

"I'm so sorry, Hanna, so sorry," she repeated, as though it were all her doing. Tears stained her collar, and when she pulled me to her, I felt her body shuddering beneath the soft fabric of her dressing gown. I pulled away. I didn't want to see her despair; I wanted her to be brave.

"I should go and pack," I said. Mother rose from the stool and shuffled into the kitchen. I retreated to the bedroom.

Erika pulled a rucksack from the closet and threw a pair of hiking boots into it. She pulled a straw sun hat from a drawer and tossed it onto her bed. I grabbed my backpack from the floor and tipped it upside down, letting the contents spill onto my mattress: a pocket flashlight, bandages, medicine, spare underwear, a packet of crackers, a can of sardines. There had been more food, but we'd eaten our way through the bag a few weeks earlier when we had been trapped in the building's basement during an air raid. I crammed the food and medicine into a suitcase, burying it under a pile of blouses, a skirt, a pair of sandals, and three pairs of underwear. How did they expect us to pack when we didn't know where we were going? I tossed in my hairbrush, then scooped it out, added a handkerchief, pulled out a skirt, and threw in a toothbrush. I left my floor-length gowns — the stiff taffetas and gossamer silks I wore when performing at the community hall — on their hangers, and my high-heeled shoes and silk gloves wrapped in their boxes of tissue paper.

"I know we have to be practical," Erika said, pulling a pale-yellow dress from the closet and draping it over my suitcase, "but you have to take this. It's your favorite."

A few weeks earlier, Mother had lugged the bolt of fabric from the attic and cut the pattern herself. She'd finished sewing the organza gown but hadn't gotten around to stitching a Star of David onto it. I was going to wear the dress Saturday night at our youth group's summer dance. I knew it was ridiculous — going to a dance in the ghetto — but it was my first dance, and Michael Wollner had asked me to partner him. *You're not going to let the Nazis stop us dancing, too, are you, Hanna?* Erika had asked. And she was right. They'd put us in the ghetto and sealed the gates; what we did inside its grimy walls was our business. I folded the dress into the suitcase.

There was still a little room left, enough for my framed photo of Clara Schumann at her piano and my leather-bound collection of her early compositions. Ever since I could remember, I'd wanted to follow in Clara's famous footsteps. When I'd turned eight, I'd convinced my parents to hire out the Debrecen Town Hall for my public debut, because Clara first performed at the age of eight. At the age of eleven, she played Chopin in Paris, so I played Chopin at the Goldmark Hall. By the age of eighteen, Clara was performing to sold-out crowds in Vienna and receiving rave reviews. I'd be turning eighteen in two and a half years.

At two in the morning, while Erika and I were still packing, my father appeared at our bedroom door with a cookie tin tucked under his arm. He reached for my hand and pulled me into the hall. Mother took Erika's arm and followed us as we went silently down the stairs and through the yard. The moon was pale, the sky gunmetal gray. Father stopped at the door to the basement, but he made no move to open it. Instead, he spun around, took five paces into the yard and stopped. He mouthed the word *five,* held up five fingers, and then stepped three paces to his left. He held his hand up again, extended three fingers and whispered the word *three*. Crouching on his heels, he lowered the battered cookie tin onto the soil and raised his hand again, extending first five fingers, then three. Satisfied that we had understood the code — and committed it to memory — he pulled a small shovel from his pants pocket and began to dig.

Father's breath was short and the back of his shirt was stained with sweat by the time he finished digging. He laid the shovel down, pried the lid from the tin, and took out a clutch of gold coins, then a wad of paper money, a handful of gems, and finally a velvet bag containing a gold pocket watch.

"There's enough here to buy you a new piano, Hanna." He smiled weakly. "And anything else you might need." He placed the velvet bag, gemstones, coins, and bills back in the tin, then lowered it into the hole. Mother reached into her apron pocket, pulled out a yarmulke and a frayed leather prayer book, and placed them on top of the tin. Finally, with trembling fingers, she pulled off her wedding band and dropped it into the hole.

We crept back to the apartment. I was glad to be inside again, seated at the kitchen table, watching my mother peel potatoes. The familiar smell of simmering cabbage was reassuring. I didn't want to think about

Father outside packing the hole with soil. I didn't want to think about digging up the ground and dusting off Mother's wedding ring. I didn't want to think about tomorrow. Erika couldn't wait to escape the ghetto. I didn't want to leave, not when I didn't know what was waiting for us outside.

Inside the ghetto walls no one called you a *dirty Jew*. There was no *us* and *them*. It was just *us* and we all wore stars, and no one had new clothes, and we all shared our bedrooms with our brothers and sisters. Nothing divided or distinguished us from one another and—like the cabbage simmering on the stove—it was comforting.

Mother had stopped crying, distracted by the task of preparing food for our journey: cheese, hard-boiled eggs, pickled cucumbers—her pantry emptied into a bag. She had once had a full pantry, its shelves fringed with white lace and bursting with preserved fruits, jams, cookies, a dozen types of tea. Mother had been happy then. Now her eyes were ringed with dark circles, and she had grown thin with worry. She cleaned incessantly. Outside, in the gutters and alleyways and front porches of the ghetto, rubbish piled up. But mother waxed and polished and dusted and swept till our apartment gleamed. I left her slicing potatoes and went back to bed.

* * *

I woke the next morning to piercing whistle blasts and the tramping of boots.

"Jews outside! Fast!" Hungarian police officers were at the end of the street, emptying apartments. Angry voices floated up through the window. A dog barked. A child screamed.

Erika was already dressed and placing the last of her belongings into her rucksack.

"You can't take that," I said, reaching for her camera. "No photos outside the ghetto—remember what Papa said? Besides, the soldiers won't let you."

"The soldiers won't know." Erika plunged the camera deep into her pack. I slipped out of my nightgown and pulled on a dress. Mother had prepared eggs for breakfast, but I couldn't eat. I sat at the piano so I wouldn't have to listen to my father's whispered prayers or watch the tears trickle down my mother's face. I'd been so naive. I'd thought we were lucky when the ghetto walls went up. Our apartment building was in the heart of the ghetto, so we didn't have to move. I still had my piano, my bed, and my family. I thought if we stayed behind the brick wall, we'd be okay.

I sat at the piano and began to play, and after a while, I forgot about the guards in the street. I forgot about the buried treasure in the backyard and Mother's bulging bag of food. I forgot about Father's big, sad eyes. I was playing piano and there was only me, the black and white keys, and Mozart.

"Hanna, grab your suitcase. It's time to go!" Father stepped into the corridor. The soldiers were outside our building.

I placed the black felt cover over the keys and closed the lid. Two weeks ago, I'd promised Piri, my piano teacher, that I would perfect Liszt's Hungarian Rhapsody no. 6 before our next lesson. Then the ghetto had been sealed, and I hadn't seen Piri since. And now we were leaving the ghetto and I couldn't practice, and that sour-faced police officer would get his sweaty hands on my piano, and I'd never match Clara Schumann's concert schedule.

"Hanna, come down at once!" Father's voice was urgent.

I thought of my piano thief and his fat fingers and his ugly smile.

"Just a minute, Papa," I called, throwing open the lid and tossing aside the felt. I ran my fingers over the keys, feeling for the one loose black key, the wobbly C-sharp Father hadn't gotten around to fixing. Pressing down on the keys either side of the C-sharp, I pulled and tugged at the key until it jerked free. Then I shoved it into my pocket and ran downstairs.

Chapter 2

We marched through the ghetto in rows of five. I could see Mr. Benedek, the kosher butcher; little Max Spitz, whom I'd babysat on weekends; old Mrs. Eppinger, bent over her walking stick; and the Markovits twins, dragging matching bags. Mother, Father, Erika, and I joined the cobbler, the fishmonger, the tailor, and the dentist.

On either side of our unhappy procession stood SS soldiers and Hungarian guards. "*Mach schnell!* Faster!" The guards raised their truncheons. Father took my suitcase. He was already carrying a rucksack on his back and the bag of food.

Outside the synagogue, a line had formed. My mother reached for my hand and we stepped into line together, snaking our way toward a convoy of open-air trucks. It was hot and my mother's hand was clammy. The pale blue fabric of her cotton dress was stained blue-black under her arms, and her hair clung to her face in matted strips. We climbed aboard the third truck and waited.

It was a relief when at midday the trucks' engines finally spluttered to life and the breeze whipped my hair dry. We'd drunk all our water, and I was thirsty and tired. I wanted to sink into sleep but there were no seats in the truck, so I stood, arms draped over the rails, facing out. I watched the wheels of the truck stir up dust clouds, into which the synagogue, and everything I'd known, disappeared.

Erika pulled her camera from her bag and a scarf from her pocket. She draped the scarf over the camera, then pulled the fabric back from the lens.

"Smile," she whispered.

I glared at her. "Just because they haven't inspected our bags doesn't mean they won't." I glanced at the camera. "Please get rid of it." But she didn't. She took photos of the guards and their guns, the trucks behind us, and the trucks in front.

"Gotcha!" she said, but she wasn't talking to me. She was talking to the guards. She was talking to Hitler.

Our convoy wound its way through the narrow streets of the ghetto and out the front gate, past the town hall and my school, the library and the park. It had been two weeks since I'd seen the fountains and domes and stained-glass windows of Debrecen Square, and I longed to jump from the truck and run through the streets. I wondered how the ducks in Debrecen Gardens were faring. No one had bread to spare.

Hatvan Street was unusually quiet for a weekday. The few people who sat at the sidewalk cafés studied their menus in silence or scurried indoors as we passed. We rumbled past a familiar cream building.

"Leo!" Father gasped.

Leo Bauer stood on his second-floor balcony, his eyes fixed on our truck, his face drained of color. The old watchmaker had worked for Father for fifteen years, until Mendel's Watch Emporium was shut down, and Leo and the rest of Father's non-Jewish employees were forced to leave their benches. The government had promised to find Leo work elsewhere, but the old man had refused.

"I know that man!" Leo pointed at my father, but the guards ignored him. "I know his family. They're good people. They've done nothing wrong." His voice echoed across the street. Behind half-drawn curtains and slanted shutters, his neighbors looked out at us, but no one stepped onto their balconies to join his protest. Leo's face crumpled. He raised his hand and waved good-bye.

A group of boys playing ball on the street moved

to the curb as our convoy rumbled past. They didn't duck into doorways or turn away. They raised their right arms.

"*Heil Hitler!*" they chanted, running after the trucks. "*Heil Hitler.*"

Erika grabbed the rails of the truck and leaned out as far as she could. Her eyes were wild, her cheeks flushed. She opened her mouth.

"Don't!" I grabbed her arm. "You'll get us shot." Erika clenched the rails; her knuckles were white. She turned back to the boys.

"Screw Hitler!" she whispered under her breath. "Screw all of you!" She let go of the rails and slumped to the floor.

We arrived at the Serly brickyards, on the outskirts of town, in the early afternoon. I clambered off the truck after my father and followed him through the gates. We weren't the first to arrive. Swarms of people from the surrounding villages and hamlets had already made their beds on the dusty dry ground. Their faces were grimy and their clothes dirty. They looked like they'd been there for days. Last year I'd camped under the stars in the Puszta Forest with Father and three friends. I could sleep outdoors again, for a few days. I looked at my father uncertainly.

"I know it seems bad," he said, "but if we stick together, we'll be okay."

Erika opened her mouth to say something. I shot her a look, and she held her tongue. Papa was trying to convince himself.

I scanned the yard. There must have been more than a thousand people crammed into the brickyard, with more pouring in. I looked at the families camped outdoors, the contents of their suitcases scattered about them. Underwear flapped in the warm wind, strung out along the barbed-wire fence. An old man, stripped to his waist, was bent over a steaming pot of water, washing himself, soaping his soft belly and the sagging skin under his arms, and all I could think was, *I want to go home; I need to go home.* He pulled a dripping rag from the bowl, loosened his belt, and reached for his zipper. I looked down at my feet. I didn't want the first naked body I saw to be old, pale, and shriveled.

We picked our way around bundles, bags, and bedrolls, looking for an empty patch of earth. I recognized a few faces — my sixth-grade teacher, the woman who worked in the post office, the Rabbi's wife — but I didn't wave or say hello.

I stepped over an elderly woman curled up on the ground and followed Father past a boy brushing his teeth over a metal bowl and a man sobbing into his prayer book.

"Let's make camp here," Father said. "At least we'll have some shelter." He set our bags down beside a disused brick kiln.

I peered inside. The ground was littered with bricks where the roof and the walls had collapsed, but there was enough room for the four of us to stretch out to sleep.

Father rolled up his pant legs, dropped to his knees, and began clearing the rubble. When the floor had been cleaned, he pulled a quilt from his bag and smoothed it over the hard concrete.

"There's room for your bags," he said, standing up and dusting himself off. I tried to smile, but it was all too sad, the crumbling shelter, my mother's awful silence, my father's forced smile. I pulled the C-sharp from my bag and hid it under my blanket. I wanted to change into clothes that didn't smell, but there was a boy on a blanket just a few feet away. He was reading a book, and his eyes kept wandering from the page. Erika smiled at him.

"He's got good taste," she whispered in my ear. She pulled the ribbon from her braid and loosened her hair so that it tumbled over her shoulders. "Let's look for a shower. My hair's filthy."

* * *

We didn't find a shower, just a dozen toilets at the far end of the brickyard, and a line that wound its way around the latrine building three times. We waited to use the toilet while others left the line in search of a tree or stone wall. Inside the block, the floors were wet with urine and the toilets jammed with soiled tissues. The place reeked. Still, it was better than squatting outside. I held my nose and crouched over the bowl.

By nightfall I was starving. Mother emptied a jar of chicken fat into a pot, and Father carried it to the fire that burned in the middle of the yard. When he returned, we dipped our bread into the melted fat and pretended we were eating fried chicken. The boy on the blanket eyed us enviously. He was drinking the watery soup the guards had doled out.

"He hasn't eaten since breakfast," Erika said, but Mother just shrugged. "His parents are dead." Erika waited for a reaction, but Mother's face stayed slack, her eyes glassy. Erika threw up her hands and walked away.

"Mother's getting worse," I whispered. My father turned away and pretended not to hear. He lifted the empty pot from the ground and busied himself cleaning it. She was losing her mind. My mother was going mad. It had started subtly. She forgot to turn off the stove; she had trouble falling asleep; she cleaned obsessively. Then she forgot street names, the names of her friends. Some days she forgot to talk at all. Father said she was tired, but it was more than that. She looked dazed. She fought it, resurfacing from the darkness from time to time to smile at us or ask about school, but the current was too strong; it kept pulling her under.

"It's late," Father said. He unbuttoned his shirt and slipped it off. "We should get some sleep." He pulled his wire-rimmed glasses from the bridge of his nose. My father had never undressed in front of me before. At home, he would loosen his tie and disappear into the bedroom to undress, reappearing the next morning for breakfast in a silk robe with a belt knotted at his waist. I hadn't seen my father in his underwear since I was six. I didn't want to see him undress. Not because I'd be embarrassed by his nakedness, but because stripped to his underwear, he'd look like everybody else. His fine linen shirt spoke of his success in business; his spectacles hinted at his love of books. In his black pants and leather belt, he was still Samuel Mendel of Mendel's Watch Emporium. Stripped to his underwear, he was just another Jew. I turned away.

Around the brickworks, fires were being put out and children put to bed. Guards prowled the perimeter fence. Father went to the toilet and Mother lay down. Erika slipped into the kiln, curled up on the floor, and closed her eyes. I tried to sleep, but I couldn't escape the smells and sounds of so many bodies so close to mine. I crawled out of bed. Father was sitting in front of the kiln cross-legged, looking up at the ink-black sky. I sat down next to him.

"Why do they hate us, Papa?"

He looked at me for a long time before answering. "It's because we're different, Hanna, and people are scared of different."

"Different?" I kept my voice low. "I have blue eyes, like them, and blond hair. I'm as smart as they are — probably smarter."

Father's voice was sad. "Your mother lights the Sabbath candles, Hanna. You walk to synagogue. To them you are a Jew and you'll always be a Jew. Be proud of that difference."

It was hard to be proud when your hair was filthy and your clothes smelled. I didn't like being different, and right at that moment, I didn't much like being a Jew.

The days passed slowly. It grew hotter and more crowded. Convoys arrived daily, and the line for the toilets grew longer. By the fifth day, all we had left was a jar of preserved plums, a piece of cheese, four pickles, and a handful of crackers. Father traded the jar of plums for a pitcher of water, and I drank from it greedily, my enjoyment tempered by the knowledge I would soon need the toilet. Erika took a sip of water and used the rest of her share to wash the dirt from her face. I was still wearing my soiled sundress. Looking down at my bare legs, at my knees crusted with mud and my toes blackened by dust, I thought of Daniel Gruber, a weedy boy fond of picking his scabs, and the first of my classmates to call me a dirty Jew. I couldn't argue with Daniel Gruber now.

Erika wanted to go for a walk. She scooped a pickled cucumber from Mother's jar, slung her camera over her shoulder, and grabbed my hand, then stepped from the kiln, dropping the cucumber into the lap of the boy on the blanket. I didn't call out or turn to tell Mother; the boy's grin was too wide. I didn't want to go with Erika — it was safer to stay out of sight — but she was going with or without me, and I couldn't let her wander the yard alone. She was bound to get into trouble. I made her promise not to photograph the guards, and we set off, picking our way through the crowd, careful not to step on a sleeping child or overturn a pot of food. We walked past toddlers playing in the dirt and mothers reading stories to their children. We saw men praying and women crying, children begging for food and people too sick to get up off the dusty ground. Those who were too tired to stand in line for soup picked through piles of rotting garbage.

Along a stretch of barbed wire, a market of sorts had been set up. Men and women trying to sell the remnants of their previous life: porcelain figurines, linen tablecloths, candelabras, schoolbooks. They didn't ask for money in return for their goods, just food. I watched an elderly man trade a crystal vase for a piece of bread, and a pregnant woman exchange a silver candlestick for a slice of beef. She nibbled at the meat and pulled a second candlestick from her bag.

"I knew Father was lying," I said, pulling the camera from Erika's face, "and you're lying, too. Those people, back there, selling their candlesticks and vases . . . Father said the war's almost over. He said we'd be home soon. So why are they selling everything?"

"Fathers lie." Erika shrugged. "It's part of the job." Erika put her hand on my arm. "He wants to protect you."

"From what?" My head was pounding. I could feel the tears welling up inside.

"Nothing." Erika smiled her big-sister smile, the one she used when she wanted to cheer me up. "Forget I said anything. I'm just tired and crabby. No one's lying.

Papa told you the war's almost over because he thinks it is."

"And what about you? What do you think?" I looked up at my sister.

"I don't know, Hanna. All I know is that I'll do whatever it takes to get home. And you're coming with me."

I wanted to go with her. I wanted to be back in our apartment, in my own room, my own bed. But Erika couldn't get us there — not on her own. I couldn't help her if Papa continued to keep the truth from me. I walked back to the brick kiln, bubbling with anger.

I wasn't a child. I was fifteen, and I needed to know what was going on. I needed a plan. That's how I'd won my place at the conservatorium. I wasn't as gifted as Magda Malek or as charming as Ilonka Bardos. I'd won my place because I worked harder and practiced more than anyone else. Magda skipped practice for parties, and Ilonka took risks, adding her own interpretation to her pieces. I played by the rules, and so far, it had worked for me. If I was going to make it back home with Erika, I needed to know where we were going and what was expected of us.

It wasn't dark when we arrived back at the kiln from our walk, but Father was already asleep. He was still wearing his black pants, but he'd taken off his shirt and was sleeping on the ground in his undershirt. My mother slept beside him, her head on his bundled shirt. They were holding hands. I didn't wake him, and later, when he slipped from the kiln and unzipped his pants to pee, I pretended I was asleep.

"We're leaving tomorrow," Father said the next morning, but he didn't sound glad. "We have to be packed and ready to go at six o'clock."

"Where are we going?"

"I don't know," Father said quietly. "I've heard mention of camps in Poland. . . ."

"Poland, Austria, Italy. What does it matter?" Mother had barely spoken the last five days. Now she spoke hurriedly, nervously, her words rushing after each other. "If they take us to a camp, at least we'll live like humans. We'll have beds and clean sheets and the floors will be swept, and if we work, they'll feed us." She rummaged through the food bag and pulled out a broken cracker, then she held the bag upside down. When nothing fell from it, she turned it inside out and shook it again. "I hear the camps in Austria are like vacation resorts. Much nicer than the ones in Poland."

I glanced at Erika. She was staring at Mother and biting her lip. She wasn't angry with her, just sad. Mother tossed the empty bag aside. "I'm sure we'll find a piano there for you, Hanna." She smiled, but she wasn't looking at me when she spoke. She was gazing out across the yard at no one in particular.

We were allowed one small bag each. I had my backpack, Mother had the empty food bag, and Father unhappily stuffed his velvet prayer bag with a change of clothes. Erika borrowed a bag from the boy on the blanket.

"How are we supposed to pack when we don't know where we're going?" I asked, opening my suitcase and running my fingers over my yellow organza gown. I pulled a clean cotton dress from under the gown and shoved it into my pack.

Erika crammed a bra, a pair of stockings, and a nightdress into her bag, before placing the camera gently inside.

Father grabbed her arm. "Not the camera, Erika. You'll be caught, and I don't want to think what they'll do to you."

Erika pried Father's fingers from her arm. "They're the ones who should be punished, Papa. We can't let them get away with this." She dropped his hand and turned back to her bag.

A tear slid down my father's cheek. He brushed it away with the back of his hand, but it was too late; I'd seen my father cry—my unflappable, courageous, strong, smart father. I reached out to him, but he didn't notice; he was looking at Erika.

"You're right," he said. "They shouldn't get away with it, but you're not going to stop them and neither will that camera. I'm sorry. It's too dangerous."

Erika brushed her lips against my father's bristly chin and lifted the camera out of the bag. "Okay, Papa."

A voice boomed over a loudspeaker. Father turned toward the noise, and Erika lowered the camera back into her bag.

I turned to Erika. "You can't take it," I began, but Father hushed me.

We were to line up immediately and take our valuables with us. I looked around, confused. We weren't meant to leave until tomorrow! Erika pointed at a cluster of tables set up in the middle of the yard. Each was manned by two Hungarian policemen. A banner hung from each table. The first bore the word PAPERS, the second PERSONAL EFFECTS, and the third VALUABLES. People were already standing in line. Those at the front were pushed toward the tables and forced to unzip their cases or tip them up. They poured their passports, family photos, and birth certificates onto the first table. The second table disappeared under cameras, fur stoles, and silk scarves. The third table was cleared every few minutes by an SS guard clutching a leather briefcase into which he piled watches, wedding bands, and coins and bills pulled from wallets and purses.

We fell into line with our bag of valuables: my letter of acceptance from the Budapest Conservatorium, the engraved silver fountain pen Mother had given me on my twelfth birthday for my bat mitzvah, Erika's final school report, and the cuff links father had worn on his wedding day. Erika said she had nothing of value to hand over, and I wasn't going to start an argument, not when we were in line. I pulled the photo of Clara Schumann in its silver frame from my suitcase and handed it to my mother along with the leather-bound book of Clara's early compositions. You couldn't tell I'd torn two pages from the book. Not unless you looked really closely.

"Excuse me, but I really must keep these," Mother said, waving our documents in front of the officers at the PAPERS table. "They're just bits of paper. They'd be of no value to you, but they're terribly important for Erika and Hanna." Mother introduced Erika and me to the officers as if they were suitors coming to tea. She was holding up the line, but the officers didn't hurry her. They seemed amused by the distraction. They bowed theatrically. Erika scowled at the men. I ignored them.

"Erika is going to apply to the university. She's very bright," Mother said earnestly. "She'll need her school report for admission." The officers began to snigger, but Mother didn't notice. *They're teasing you,* I wanted to yell at her. *They're laughing at you. Please. Stop.* But she didn't.

"And Hanna here." She put her arm around me. "She'll be taking up her position as a soloist at the Budapest Conservatorium."

Father reached over and took my mother's elbow in his hand. He looked worried. "Mira," he whispered gently, "enough."

But my mother didn't seem to hear. She pulled free of my father's grip, apologized to the smaller of the two officers—a stout man with a sunburned nose—and handed him my letter of acceptance. The officer inspected the notice and handed it to his partner with a wink.

He turned to my mother. "Most impressive. Unfortunately, we can't let you keep your papers. We could put them in safekeeping, though."

"Yes!" Mother clapped her hands. "That would be wonderful! They'll be much safer with you. You keep them until we return."

A cruel smile split the officer's face, but Mother had already moved on. She was holding up my silver fountain pen and talking to the officers at the next table.

The next day, we marched through the front gates of the brickyard, a long line of Jews with sacks on our backs. We no longer had pets, iceboxes, bicycles, beds, pianos, or photo albums. We had crumbs in our pockets and, if we were lucky, water. Most of us carried underwear, socks, and a toothbrush. Erika had a camera. I had Clara's Piano Concerto in A Minor and a black C-sharp.

My feet ached in my strappy sandals, but we weren't allowed to stop. Those who begged for water or stopped to catch their breath were forced back into line with the butt of a rifle. I heard a voice cry out and turned back to look. The boy from the blanket had tripped over a rock. He lay on the ground, clutching his ankle, while a guard stood over him, holding a gun. *Get up!* I wanted to shout. *Get up or they'll shoot.* But I didn't call out. I turned back and kept my eyes trained on the back of my father's head. You didn't yell or fight back or step out of line here. You did as you were told. You put one foot in front of the other, and you kept your head down. You marched in time and shut out everything else: your thirst, your aching legs, the screams. I counted my steps in 4/4 time—one-two-three-four, over and over, like a metronome, blocking out everything except the beat. Just as Piri had taught me.

We arrived at a train station in the early afternoon, but it wasn't a station that I'd been to before. I stepped into line behind my father and inched forward slowly, past cargo wagons and freight cars. Across the tracks, on another platform, a passenger train was idling. Its compartments were empty, except for the dining cabin, where an SS officer sat drinking tea with his wife and daughter. The young girl wore a cream-colored shirt with a lace collar and a straw hat with a matching ribbon. Her hair was set in waves, and her lips were painted pink. She was reading a book.

We didn't cross the tracks to board the train. We stopped at the mouth of a cattle car, an empty slatted box without seats or windows. I faltered, confused, but the swell of the line carried me up and in, after my parents and sister. A hundred bodies piled in after us, on top of us, pressed against the walls of the wagon and crammed into its corners. The cattle car groaned, and when we couldn't be packed in any tighter, its heavy door was closed and nailed shut.

Outside, children screamed, dogs barked, and soldiers shouted. Inside, it was dark.

Chapter 3

The train car smelled like a toilet. I held my nose and fought the urge to throw up. Erika and I pushed through the crush of bodies to get to a small grate at the far end. We took turns at the wall, tilting our heads up toward the little air that filtered through the slats.

A bucket sat in a corner, its lumpy contents spilling onto the floor. When I couldn't hold on any longer, Father held his coat up and I squatted behind it, but Mother refused to go. "I don't have any toilet paper," she fretted. "I'll just hold on until we reach the next station."

But there was no next station. Through the slats of the grate I saw fragments of sky, scraps of green, and flashes of gray—station platforms with strange-sounding names. We'd passed dozens already. The sky had grown dark and then lightened again, and we still hadn't stopped.

I opened my backpack.

"Anyu, I found some toilet paper. Take it; you're in pain."

Father held up his coat again and Mother crouched behind it, clutching the first page of Clara's Concerto in A Minor. I didn't need the sheet music to play Clara's pieces. I knew all her concertos by heart. I just wanted the crotchets and semiquavers for company, a reminder of the life I'd return to once we were free.

"Remember when we used to sit in the air-raid shelter?" Erika pulled me close. "It was dark and cramped and we'd sit there for hours, and Papa would tell his corny jokes and Anyu would sing. And when the siren finally sounded and we opened the door, remember how good the sun felt on our faces?"

I closed my eyes and pictured my sister and me lying on the grass, our faces turned up to the summer sun. When Erika brushed against me, her body wasn't sticky with sweat; it was slick with suntan oil, and the stifling heat in the wagon was another summer's day, and the clank of the wheels was a song on the radio.

I fell asleep. When I woke, Michael Wollner was standing next to me.

"Sorry—did I wake you? It's hard to see in here, and you were standing against the wall. I thought you were awake. . . ." His breath smelled like sour milk.

"It's okay," I said, rubbing my eyes. "I'm awake.

What time is it?"

"I don't know." He stood on his toes and peered through the grate. "It's dark outside."

"Dark? That means we've been traveling for two days."

Michael nodded. "Tonight's the night we were going to have the dance. . . ." Even in the half-light, I could see his face flush. Michael stared at his feet. I picked at my hem. The dance was to have been held in an unheated hall in the ghetto. There would have been no food and no decorations and yet I'd been excited. Nervous, too, to have a boy's arms around my waist for the first time, and his mouth at my neck. Now we were breathing down each other's necks and we were all clammy and a school dance sounded wonderful.

"Mother sent me over to ask if you could spare some water." He held out a cup. "We've run out, and she can't take her medicine. I wouldn't ask, but she's feeling faint." I opened our flask and poured a few drops into his cup.

"I hope she feels better," I said, tucking the flask back into our bag. Michael returned to his mother.

The car grew quiet. People were too weak and hungry to fight over floor space. Every time the train lurched to a stop, we were thrown against the walls and battered by damp bodies. Whatever bleak thoughts the adults had they kept to themselves. Occasionally, Mother would hum a tune to herself, but her voice didn't cheer me. I just wanted to get out. Whatever our destination, it had to be better than being imprisoned in this wooden box.

Someone lit a candle. In the flickering light I saw a woman lying on the floor. Her face was gray. I'd heard bodies slump to the floor, but I'd imagined they were sleeping, at worst unconscious.

I pulled at my father's coat. "Please, Papa, cover her up." But he couldn't.

A young girl of three or four was sitting beside the lifeless body, holding its hand.

"Wake up, Mama," the girl said. She dropped her mother's hand and shook her by the shoulder, tears welling in her eyes. "Wake up, Mama. Wake up!"

"Here, take this." I handed the child page two of Clara Schumann's Concerto. "You can color it in. These notes are black." I pointed to the crotchets. "The other notes need coloring." I rummaged through Erika's bag and found a tube of red lipstick. "You can use this." The girl's eyes widened. She wiped her nose on her sleeve and took the lipstick.

"Mama's asleep." She put a finger to her lips. "It will be a surprise."

* * *

It must have been midnight on the third night when the train's wheels finally ground to a halt. A young boy who'd had his nose pressed to the grate announced we were in Poland, in a place called Auschwitz-Birkenau. The doors were flung open, and we were ordered to step onto the platform. I had longed for the sun, but after three days in the dark, the bright lights stung my eyes. It was cold, too, but the rush of clean air was a relief. Someone shouted at us to leave our bags in the train car. I pulled the C-sharp from my backpack, tucked it into the elastic of my underpants, and stepped off the train behind Erika. Father helped Mother to her feet and lifted her off the train, steadying her between us. We slipped our arms through hers and stepped into the crush of people spilling onto the platform.

Auschwitz-Birkenau. It was an odd-sounding name for a town. And an odd-looking station, too, manned by SS guards and stooped porters in filthy blue and white rags. There were no street lamps at Birkenau, only floodlights. No wooden seats, just barbed wire and men with whips and a strange hovering smog. Something huge and heavy and black moved through me.

A searchlight swept the platform, and I saw Michael Wollner jump from the train. He took his mother's hand and helped her down. Her face shone with sweat; his was grimy. A soldier brushed past them, dragging a dead body after him.

We were ordered to form two lines. Men were sent to the right, women, children, and the elderly to the left. My mother stepped to the left in confused obedience, but Father pulled her back, tears spilling onto his stubbled cheeks. He kissed her on the mouth. Then he turned to me.

"Be brave, darling Hanna, and be careful." He cupped my face in his hands and kissed me on the forehead. His lips were cracked; his stubble stung.

"You said we had to stick together, Papa. You said we'd be okay as long as we —"

"Men to the right!" an SS officer shouted, putting his gun back into its holster. Behind him a woman was slumped over her husband, cradling his bloodied face in her arms.

His lashes heavy with tears, Father turned to Erika. "Look after each other," he whispered, "and get home safe. And when you do, tell everyone what you saw and what they did to us."

And then he was gone, another pair of marching feet swallowed up by the night.

I took my mother's hand and stepped into line behind Erika.

"Your nails!" Mother scolded, looking at my hands

with horror. "You can't sit at the piano with hands like that. I want your nails cut tonight."

I wanted to slap her. I wanted to scream, *They've taken Father! Open your eyes!* but it was too late; Mother had already gone. She wasn't sad and she wasn't scared. She was back in Debrecen and her daughters were making mischief and her husband was at work.

One of us had made it home already.

Erika watched the ghosts in striped uniforms unload luggage from the trains.

"You did the right thing leaving the camera on the train," I whispered in her ear. "Photos of this would only get us in trouble."

Erika didn't answer.

"You did leave the camera on the train?" My heart dipped.

"Yes. I promised Papa I'd get rid of it if things got dangerous, and I did. But this —" Erika looked down, unfurling her right hand to reveal a metal film canister, "— this, we didn't talk about."

"You with the blond hair. How old are you?" A man with a shaved skull and a weeping eye stepped into the line beside me. He wore the same striped rags as the porters, and a yellow star was stitched over his left breast.

"Fifteen."

"You're sixteen." He looked me in the eye and spoke slowly. "Remember. Sixteen." And then he was gone.

Mother, Erika, and I neared the front of the line. A tall man in a long black leather coat was directing the women and children in front of us to his right or left. He had dark stony eyes and perfectly parted hair. In his gloved hand he held a stick, which he wielded like a baton. He reminded me of the conductor of the Budapest Philharmonic Orchestra.

Erika turned to me. "That officer just sent that woman with the limp to the left—that little boy, too. If you're an adult and you're fit, he points you to the right," she whispered, taking a step forward. "If you're a kid or you're sick, he sends you to the left, to those factories over there." She pointed to a cluster of low brick buildings.

"So, the left is factory work," I whispered, "and the right . . . hard labor?"

In front of us, the young girl from the cattle car stood before the podium, the tube of red lipstick clutched tightly in her hand. The conductor glanced at her, raised his baton, and pointed to the left.

"Anyu and I will be sent to work outdoors. We won't have a choice," Erika said quickly. "You do. Say you're fifteen."

I looked to my left, at the row of squat buildings,

the last of which belched smoke from a giant chimney. The sky had grown light and I was dizzy with hunger. I thought of mother's stove top and the fried eggs she'd cooked for me the morning we'd left the ghetto, and how I'd left them on my plate, untouched. Maybe I'd be put to work in the factory; maybe soon I'd be fed.

We stepped up to the podium. The conductor beckoned Mother and Erika forward.

"I'll find you," Erika whispered, pulling her hand from mine. The conductor glanced at them and waved his wand to the right. Mother didn't turn around to say good-bye.

It was my turn. I blotted the sweat from my face with my sleeve and stepped forward. The conductor took one of my braids in his gloved hand and smiled.

"Goldenes haar." He looked into my eyes. His voice was smooth, a honeyed baritone. *"Bist du Judin?"* I nodded. Yes, I was a Jew.

"Wie alt bist du?"

I opened my mouth. The conductor wanted to know how old I was.

I was directed to join the women on the other side of the podium. Erika frowned when she saw me. "You said you were sixteen?"

I nodded. "I couldn't leave you to look after Mother

alone," I said. But I was lying. Erika didn't need me. I needed her. I needed my big sister to keep looking out for me. Father couldn't, Mother wouldn't, and I didn't know how to take care of myself. Not here.

Erika took my hand and I took Mother's, and together we walked toward a sign that read WORK CAMP, and through a door marked RECEPTION BLOCK. A large grim woman with a green triangle on her dress took our names and told us to wait. Dozens of women waited beside us. The summer sun shone through the windows and seeped through the walls, and the room grew hot. The sound of a dripping tap echoed across the room. A note above the tap warned against drinking the water. A woman cupped her hands under the spout.

"Kannst du nicht lesen, du idiot!" A girl with a green triangle on her dress and mud-colored eyes grabbed the woman by the back of her collar and yanked her from the sink. "Can't you read?" she yelled, and then she punched her. *"Wer kann Deutsch?"* She swung around to address us, wiping her bloodied fist in the folds of her skirt. She wanted to know who among us spoke German. I'd studied the language at school, but I kept my head down. A woman in front of me put up her hand.

"*Gut.* You'll interpret. Now tell these whores to undress."

Undress? I froze. *In front of each other?*

Mother peeled off her stockings while the women around her fumbled with their buttons and slipped off their shoes. Erika stepped out of her dress and left it puddled on the floor. I closed my eyes. *When I open them, this will all be a bad dream.*

"Move it!" the interpreter yelled. I pulled my crumpled dress over my head, crossed my arms over my chest, and hoped no one would notice that I was still wearing my underwear. Ever since I'd gotten my period, I'd undressed behind locked doors. Mother hadn't seen my changed body, and I was still getting used to it — to the curve of my hips and my rounded breasts and the soft blond hair between my legs.

A skinny girl wearing a sacklike dress and a yellow star walked between us, scooping up bras, stockings, underwear, and dresses. She pointed a bony finger at my groin. "I'll get in trouble if you're wearing those. Take them off or I'll call the guards."

"Don't call them," I begged. "I'll take them off right now. See?" I pulled the C-sharp from my waistband, stepped out of my underpants, and let them fall to the floor.

We were herded into a hall. Five women with razors, soap brushes, and scissors stormed into the room. Mother had to be held down by three of them, but when it was my turn, I didn't struggle. I leaned forward and closed my eyes and let them hack at my hair. And when my braids hit the floor, I let the women scrape at my scalp with a razor. They shaved my head, my legs, and my underarms. Then they shaved off my pubic hair.

"Don't let them see you cry." Erika blotted the tears from my face. "It's only hair. It'll grow back."

I didn't need a mirror to see what I looked like. A hundred mirror images stood in the room with me: hairless, wild-eyed, dirty, and shivering. We were the bald prisoners in rags I'd seen at the station. And the lingering smog that smelled so foul? The bluish clouds that rose from the giant chimney? They weren't cooking breakfast. They were burning hair.

We marched, single file, from one hall to another, but the guards didn't seem to notice our nakedness, or our tears. They looked through us — as if we were transparent — and somehow that was worse. We were in a cavernous room with showerheads in the ceiling. I balled my hand around my C-sharp.

"Your film will get wet," I whispered to Erika.

"I slipped it under a step when we walked in," she

whispered back, and I remembered the step and her stumbling over it and the women behind us grumbling to pass.

They were grumbling now and looking up at the showerheads. Some were crying. The Markovits twins huddled in a corner of the room, holding hands. A woman with drooping breasts and veined legs sat naked on the concrete floor, reciting Kaddish, the prayer for the dead.

"Aren't they glad to get clean?" I asked, but Erika didn't answer. When the water pelted down, she turned her face up to the ceiling and scrubbed the dirt from her body. I watched the brown rivers of dirt trickle down her legs and disappear down the drain and wished I could disappear, too. Mother stood quietly beside us, her eyes closed, her head tilted up to the water, massaging her hairless scalp with her fingertips, as if she were at home in her bathroom. I lifted my mouth to the showerhead. The water tasted like it came from a swamp, but I didn't spit it out.

We were handed drab gray dresses with yellow triangles, worn underwear, and a pair of hard wooden clogs. We weren't given a towel. I slipped the dress over my dripping body and slid my feet into the shoes.

Erika's clogs didn't fit, so she handed them to the guard and asked for another pair. The guard laughed and said, "Try this on for size." The rest happened so quickly—the guard's raised arm, the tip of her whip sailing toward my sister's face, Erika recoiling, leather catching skin, my sister's torn cheek, her small, thin cry. I stood there, mute.

We were herded into another room, and I was pushed into a chair. My wrists were pinned down, and someone jabbed me with a needle, piercing the pale fleshy underside of my arm, over and over until, beneath the blood, I could make out a number in blue ink: A10573. Nothing belonged to me anymore—not my piano, my home, my name, or my hair. I was a number now.

Someone wiped a bloodied rag across my arm and pointed to the door. I rose from the chair, careful not to drop my C-sharp. I looked down at the black key resting in my palm and at my long, slender fingers and the freckles on my arms.

I'm still Hanna Mendel, I said to myself. *I'm five foot seven. I have a birthmark on my left shoulder. I'm scared of spiders. I'm hopeless at sports. I like Clara Schumann, and one day I'm going to be famous.*

Chapter 4

We walked past endless rows of identical gray buildings until we reached our barrack. A woman was waiting for us outside. She wore a scarf over her shaved head, and she carried a whip. She looked mean. She introduced herself as our block leader and ordered us into the wooden shed. The windowless room looked like a barn and smelled like a kennel. The walls were bare and the floor was grimy. A row of narrow bunks spread across two walls: wooden planks in three tiers, so close together that if you sat up, you'd scrape your head on the tier above. There were no mattresses on the planks, just thin gray blankets.

"Welcome to your new home." The block leader kicked the door closed. I looked at the splintering bunks and the crumbling walls. There was nothing of my home here, and with every minute that passed, there was less of me. I flopped onto a bunk.

"Rule number one: no sitting." The block leader cracked her whip, and I leaped off the bunk. There were no Nazi guards stalking the barrack, no SS watching from the door. I glanced at the block leader, her bony arms folded across her chest, her eyes stony. She was wearing a yellow star—she was one of us.

"Rule number two," she continued in her thick Polish accent. "If there's anything hidden under your blankets: an apple core, a spoon, soap"—she pulled a blanket from a bunk, sending a family of bugs scuttling—"there will be consequences."

My mother pulled at my sleeve. "Hanna, where's the kitchen?"

The block leader glared at my mother. "Rule number three." She stepped toward us and rammed a finger against my mother's lips. "No talking." She pressed her forefinger and thumb on either side of my mother's trembling mouth and clamped her lips shut. "Understand?"

My mother nodded, her eyes wide with fright. The block leader smiled, pulled her fingers from Anyu's mouth, and wiped her hand across my mother's skirt.

"Next time you interrupt, I'll knock your teeth out." She paused for effect. "Rule number four: you'll be fed three times a day. Coffee at five a.m., soup for lunch, and bread for dinner. If you're lucky, you'll get margarine."

The block leader pointed to a battered cardboard box on the floor.

"Take a cup. Look after it. You lose the cup, you go hungry."

I pulled a rusted cup from the box and, copying the woman next to me, threaded the worn belt from my dress through the cup's handle, so that my cup hung at my waist.

The block leader ordered us outside and told us to form a single line. We marched in silence, past numbered buildings and nameless roads, until we reached a block marked LATRINES. A woman lunged for the door, clutching her stomach, but the block leader barred her way. "No one enters without a guard." She scowled, shoving the door open to reveal a deep pit dug into the earth. She pointed to the woman. "You! Wait till last. The rest of you . . . time to shit."

We walked from the latrines to a dusty square, where we were made to wait for hours in the burning sun so the guards could count us. I looked at my mother, at her caved-in face and vacant eyes. She'd been pretty once. Now she looked worn. Next to her stood a woman with blistering skin, her pink face shiny with sweat, and beyond her, more pinched faces and frightened eyes.

The sun collapsed, and the sky grew dark. We

returned to our hut. Dinner was a slice of black bread and a square of margarine, which we smeared across the bread with our fingers. The bread tasted like mud, but I forced it down. I climbed into a bunk between Erika and Mother. Three women squeezed in after us. I was too tired for introductions. I closed my eyes, but I couldn't sleep. The bed was too hard and the room too quiet. I thought of the villages and homes we'd passed in the cattle train, and the people inside them sleeping on clean sheets under blankets. They had food and water and clean clothes. They went to school and played piano. It had been seven days since I'd sat at my piano. I hadn't missed a day's practice since I was seven. I slipped my C-sharp from the frayed elastic of my secondhand underwear and rubbed its soft, worn wood.

Mother turned to look at me. "Play something for me, Hanna." Angry voices shouted at Mother to shut up, but she kept talking. "What about Liszt? Piri will be here tomorrow, and you've hardly practiced." A flashlight clicked on at the far end of the hut. Feet slid into shoes. I had to keep Mother quiet.

"I'll play, but be quiet, Anyu. Please." I moved my trembling fingers up and down my mother's back. I played Mozart and Bartok while horrible, hungry tears rolled down my face. I was tapping out Chopin's Fifth

Étude when the block leader walked past. I froze. If she passed the beam of her flashlight over us, we'd be hauled out of bed, but if I stopped drumming on my mother's back, Anyu was sure to complain. I forced my fingers to continue. The block leader walked the length of the room three times, then went back to bed. I began my next piece.

"I know this one. What is it, Hanna?" Mother asked excitedly.

"It's Liszt's Hungarian Rhapsody," I whispered, my heart splintering into a thousand pieces. "Your favorite."

"And beautifully played. Piri will be so pleased with your progress." Mother yawned.

I fell into a bitter sleep and woke to the sound of shouting. A bell was ringing, and girls were frantically jumping from their bunks and pulling on their shoes. I leaped from my bunk, smoothed my blanket over the rough wooden planks, and followed Erika to the washroom. Women ran past us. One woman urinated as she ran, a slow, wet trail dribbling down her inside thigh. No one wanted to miss breakfast.

"You'll be showered and shaved once a month." The block leader stood at the door. "Until then, unless you want to smell like a sewer rat, I suggest you find yourselves a tap. You may want to wash your underwear, too." She lifted a pair of underpants from the muddy floor and flung them at the woman who had discarded them. "You won't get another clean pair for a month." She addressed the room again. "And if you wash them, you better have them back on before breakfast. There'll be no whores in my block parading around without underwear."

Her scarf came loose, and she pushed it away from her face with the back of her muddy hand, leaving a smear of brown dirt across her pink forehead. Erika and I looked at each other. We both opened our mouths. *Pig.* I mouthed the word first. It was a game Erika and I had played since we were children. Mr. Halasz, our principal, looked like a bear, and Mrs. Beck, from apartment 10C, resembled a mouse. Erika had names for all the children at school she disliked: bulging-eyed Max Szabo was the Goldfish and Ida Stern, the Piranha because of her teeth. The block leader looked like a pig: the angry pink face covered in mud, the broad nose like a snout, the black beady eyes. *Pig* was perfect.

I looked at the women fighting to stand over the rusted basins. Stripped naked, they bent over the cracked porcelain, struggling to scour the dirt from their bodies without soap.

I turned to leave.

"You're not washing?" Erika asked.

My skin felt itchy, my scalp, too, but it all seemed like a waste of energy, washing our faces with festering water, drying ourselves with our dirty dresses.

"I can't see the point."

"The point is to stay human." Erika bent over a bowl of brown water and splashed her face. "We mustn't become animals, Hanna. That's what they want."

I walked back to the barrack with the Markovits twins. At school I'd always been able to tell them apart. Lili wore her hair swept up in a ponytail. Her ribbons were blue. Agi preferred pink and always wore braids. Now they were bald. I looked from one to the other.

"I'm Lili. That's Agi," Lili said, pointing to her sister. "Don't feel bad; even we get confused."

"Did you lie to get in here, too?" I whispered, looking over my shoulder to see whether the block leader had followed us out.

"Lie? About what?" The twins looked confused.

"The man with the stick — he was sending children to the left and adults to the right. I said I was sixteen so I could stay with Erika."

"He didn't ask us our age," Lili answered for both of them.

"But he asked lots of questions about us being identical twins," Agi butted in. "He was so excited, you'd think he'd never seen a pair of twins."

We stopped talking when the block leader returned from the washroom. I lined up with my tin cup behind Lili and Agi and waited for breakfast. I got a splash of cold black water and gulped it down. The block leader called it coffee, but it tasted like dishwater. A thin woman with peeling lips was bent over her cup, crying. The block leader put down her ladle.

"She doesn't eat, so no one eats." The block leader grabbed the pot of black water, kicked open the door, and hurled it outside. The woman looked up from her rusted cup.

"You want something to cry about?" The block leader glowered. "Outside! Now!"

The woman stood up and walked to the door. Her skirt was wet, but I couldn't tell if it was coffee or fear that stained the fabric. The block leader followed her out, and the door slammed shut behind them. I looked about frantically. We weren't allowed to cry? What else weren't we allowed to do? No one met my gaze. The few women who had coffee tipped their cups up and drank hurriedly before the block leader returned. A girl was bent over in the middle of the room, her nose to the floor, sucking at the black drops that had dripped from the pot. Those without breakfast stared angrily at the door.

"Bitch," someone whispered, but they weren't

talking about the block leader. They were talking about the woman who'd cried into her cup.

We lined up again, bookended by two women with green triangles and truncheons. My stomach grumbled.

"Work detail!" the block leader announced when she returned to the room, red-faced and panting. The woman with the peeling lips wasn't behind her. "You're here to work. Work and you'll be fed."

"What work will we be doing?" Erika asked, nervously eyeing the block leader's whip. Her fingers fluttered to her face. Her cheek was still swollen. Her skin raw.

"Ditch digging, carting rocks, whatever you're told. If you can sew or cook or do anything else useful with your hands, let me know and I'll get you a job."

Erika and I looked at Mother, then at each other. Mother could sew and cook, but we couldn't let her out of our sight. She no longer knew what she was saying or where she was. If she stayed with us, we could protect her.

"There are easier jobs I can recommend you for." The block leader lowered her voice. "All I expect in return is a small token of your appreciation." She pulled a cigarette from her pocket and slipped it between her yellowing teeth.

We walked through the main gate, joined by other

groups of weary women and a dozen armed guards. I thought I heard a violin amid the clatter of wooden shoes, and then the clash of symbols and the beat of a drum, but when I looked around, there was nothing but mud, and the farther we marched, the fainter the noise grew. We walked for an hour along dirt roads and through fields until we reached a quarry. The guards formed a sentry around a huge pit and ordered prisoners with whips to stand at the lip of the hole.

"*Los! Schnell!* Into the pit!" The guards raised their guns and fired into the air. I scratched my knee, scrambling down the rock face, but I didn't cry—a prisoner with a whip was watching me, a smile on her lips. I wondered what they'd done to her to make her change sides.

"They've dug our graves," the woman next to me cried out. "We're all going to die!"

"Nonsense," said Mother quickly. "We're here to work."

Erika was paired with Mother, and I helped a Polish girl with blistered ears.

"I've carted rocks for two years, and I'm still stronger than you," she complained when, for the second time, I dropped a load of rocks. "You won't last a week."

You think I want to be here? I wanted to yell.

Just beyond the quarry there was a forest of fir trees.

Less than five minutes by foot, but it might as well have been ten miles. There was no escaping the quarry. There were a dozen guards with guns, and dogs circling the pit. If we tried to run, the block leader had warned, we'd be hunted down, and when we were found, ten of our bunk mates would be shot for our crime.

We stopped for lunch when the sun was overhead. The cabbage soup was gritty, but I licked the bowl clean. We dragged ourselves back to camp at nightfall. My scalp was burned, my feet were blistered, and my arms felt like lead. When we neared the main gate, I noticed the group quicken its pace. And then I heard music — the muffled beat of a drum and the clanging of cymbals, and that violin that had sung in my head. The sounds grew louder and more insistent as we approached the gate.

"A band!" Mother was wide-eyed as we marched past the watchtower. Just inside the main gate stood a welcoming committee — a band of prisoners in white collars and blue skirts, with violins tucked under their chins. They had sheet music and accordions, drums and cymbals. They were belting out a march. The prisoners forced their tired legs up and down in time to the hypnotic 4/4 beat. I missed my piano more than my bed, but this wasn't music. This was grotesque.

* * *

As the summer months passed, I learned to block out the music and a lot else besides. I learned to keep very quiet and still when all I wanted to do was cry and scream and run. I learned that to care was weak and brutality a virtue in this upside-down world. I learned to hold a hand under my chin while eating bread so I didn't waste the crumbs and to sleep holding my shoes and my cup so they wouldn't be stolen. I learned to hang back in the food line because vegetables settled at the bottom of the pot. I learned that the fat get fed and the hungry stay hungry. I learned that political prisoners wore red triangles, homosexuals wore pink, and murderers boasted green — and the green triangles were the women you didn't cross.

I got used to the smell of the latrines and the hard beds and the endless roll calls, but the gnawing hunger never eased. When the block leader was out of earshot, Erika and I would play games to trick our stomachs into thinking they were full. We'd plan sumptuous dinner parties and describe every dish in intricate detail, clutching our bellies and complaining because we were too full.

The days were difficult, but the nights were worse. In Debrecen, I'd dreamed of performing in Paris. In Birkenau, I dreamed of Papa. I knew my father would be okay. He'd been the finest watchmaker in Debrecen, and our block leader said there was work for those who were skilled with their hands. It was just that I missed him. I missed my mother, too — the mother I knew before the war. The one who sang me to sleep at night and never tired of watching me practice. The mother who washed my tangled hair every Saturday night and helped me with my algebra. The Mira Mendel who spoke four languages and sewed all my concert gowns by hand.

I thought of Piri often. I wondered whether she'd looked for me after the ghetto had been emptied. Piri had taught piano at my school for fifteen years, quitting when the principal stopped music classes for Jews. She taught me privately after that, cycling into the ghetto once a week with her satchel of sheet music. She brought Liszt and Chopin, but she also smuggled in Goldschmidt and Krenek and jazz music, even though it was banned. Piri couldn't stand bigots.

I was thinking about my teacher when we were forced to congregate in the main square of Birkenau. I'd thought it strange that our barrack was invited to attend a concert, perverse even, given that the audience was composed of prisoners who had no choice but to attend. The conductor smiled at the guards seated in the front row and introduced her ensemble as the Birkenau Women's Orchestra. Most of them wore yellow stars; all had scarves on their heads, white blouses, and pleated skirts. I recognized the violinist from the Budapest Philharmonic Orchestra. The woman sitting next to her was a famous flautist from France. Then Piri stepped into the spotlight.

What was my teacher doing here? She wasn't Jewish. And why was she playing for the guards? She despised the SS. The conductor raised her baton, and Piri hunched over the piano. The conductor tapped at the lectern, and Piri's fingers flew to the keys. She played Schubert, then Strauss, her performance flawless but cold.

The conductor took her final bow, and we were ordered back to the barrack. When the block leader stopped to congratulate the conductor, I slunk to Piri's side.

"Piri, what are you doing here?" I pulled her behind a group of inmates.

"Hanna! I've been looking for you everywhere. When I didn't see you, I worried that you'd been —"

I didn't let her finish her sentence, I had too many questions.

"Why are you here, Piri?"

"Because I'm 'sympathetic to the cause.'" She pointed to the red triangle on her striped shirt and rolled her eyes. "I teach Jews to play piano, so I'm politically dangerous."

"How can you do it?" I asked, pulling away from her. "Play for them? Entertain them? I want to scratch their eyes out."

Piri looked at me sadly.

"I want to survive. Orchestra members get extra rations. We don't have to work."

"Neither do the girls in barrack 24 who part their legs for the guards."

"I want to get out of here alive, and I won't apologize for it, Hanna."

The block leader called our barrack to attention.

"I can get you into the orchestra. There's room for another pianist. Think about it," Piri said, slipping back into line. "We're in barrack 14."

"It's the only way to beat them," Erika said when I told her about my conversation with Piri. "Survive, and when you do, tell everyone what you saw—"

"And what they did to us," I said, remembering Father's parting words. "I just don't know if I could live with myself." I thought of the girls in barrack 24, their hair grown out, their lips painted red. I'd seen the guards go in there at night and come out again, buttoning their flies and straightening their shirts.

"Do it for Anyu, then. You could give her your extra rations. She barely escaped the last selection. If she gets any frailer, they'll take her away."

I watched my mother drag her feet through the mud. In two days, the guards would force us to hop up and down at the next selection so they could pick off the weakest among us. Last week a woman had tripped; another had collapsed. They were taken by the guards and hadn't come back.

I slipped away the next morning, after the block leader left for the washroom. I ran to Piri's barrack and knocked on the door. No one answered, so I swung the door open and stepped inside. A stove was burning in the corner of the room, a pot of coffee bubbling on the flame. I closed my eyes for a moment and inhaled, the smell tugging me back to our kitchen in Debrecen.

There were beds with straw pallets, blankets, and sheets, and at the foot of each bed, there was a small washbasin and soap. Farther along the wall was a podium cluttered with music stands and a wooden table buried under sheet music. I didn't stop to look at the music; I walked straight to the piano.

I'd never played a Bechstein before. I ran my fingers over the keys, and the music reached out to me like an old friend. I flirted with Schubert and waltzed with

Chopin. By the time I was halfway through Clara Schumann's Second Scherzo, I was lost to the music. It seeped into the corners of the barrack and slipped under the sheets. The bunks blurred at the edges and the bars on the windows disappeared as the melody wrapped its arms around me and carried me away.

I didn't hear the door open. I didn't know I had an audience until a cymbal skimmed past the piano and clattered to the floor. I looked up from the keys. The conductor of the women's orchestra was standing at the door. Behind her was Piri.

"Who the hell are you?" The conductor reached for a bar of soap and flung it at my head. I ducked for cover behind the piano's sloping lid. "Get away from that piano!"

I slid from the seat and crouched on the floor.

"Frau Schroeder, if I may." Piri stepped forward and faced the conductor. "This is Hanna Mendel, one of my students from Debrecen."

I stood up and faced the conductor. My hands were shaking.

"She's a talented pianist and—" Piri was pale.

"I don't recall asking you to find me a musician." The conductor took a step toward Piri. "Did I?"

"No, Frau Schroeder, but I thought—"

The conductor slammed the piano lid shut.

"I have no need for her." She brought her face close to Piri's. "And if she isn't out of here by the time I sit down, I'll call for the guards."

I got back to the barrack just as the women were leaving for the quarry. I slipped into line behind my mother.

"I'm joining the Birkenau Women's Orchestra," I whispered in her ear. I needed to see her smile.

"That's wonderful, darling. You'll get to practice. You must keep practicing." My mother smiled, but her eyes were sad.

"Of course, Anyu." I took her hand in mine. It was tiny as a child's. She opened her mouth to speak, but a terrible sound ripped through the barrack, a deep rumbling, then a low growl. The floor shook, and our plank beds with it, and through the cracks in the barrack walls, we saw the sky turn red.

My mother turned to face me. "Maybe you'll play a little Clara Schumann for me when you get out of here." Her eyes searched mine. "Hanna," she said, "don't ever give up."

I thought she was talking about the piano, but the way she looked at me made me think she was talking about something entirely different.

Chapter 5

"A10562! A10563!" Lili and Agi Markovits stepped forward. "You're excused from today's selection. You're to meet Herr Mengele at the infirmary."

Agi smiled. Herr Mengele had promised he would call for them, and the twins had since found out that the man they had called the conductor was an SS captain and a doctor. In Birkenau, they'd learned, it was all about who you knew.

"A10573!" I stepped forward. "You're wanted in block 11."

A guard opened the door and ushered me into a shower block. I'd showered twice since coming to the camp, but never in a room with shower cubicles and towels. A woman at the far end of the room stepped out of a cubicle, her hair dripping. She pulled a dress with a green triangle from a hook on the wall and slipped it over her head.

The guard pressed her gun into my back. There were five girls wearing yellow stars standing in the middle of the room. I hurried to join them.

None of them turned to look at me. They stood, silent and still, staring down at their feet or blinking nervously at the door. I turned to the girl next to me. I knew that face, those eyes . . . The girl was bald, and skinnier than I remembered, but she had the same pale, freckled face as the shy third-year pianist at the Budapest Conservatorium who stuttered when she spoke but made the keys dance when she touched them. Her name was Rivka Hermann. Rivka glanced up, but she didn't look at me. Lagerführerin Holzman was striding toward us, flanked by two guards.

"Permit me to introduce myself," the *Lagerführerin* began, but she needn't have. We all knew the commander. She was head of the women's camp, the most powerful woman in Auschwitz-Birkenau. Women trembled when they talked of her and dipped their heads when she passed. She sat down on a bench and crossed her silk-stockinged legs. I stood in front of her in my gray sack dress, my fingernails caked with dirt.

"I have good news for one of you," she began, but I didn't look up. I'd seen her standing at the camp gate waiting for someone to turn and look at her. I'd seen too many girls make the mistake and be pulled out of line, never to be seen again. "The commandant of the camp, Captain Jager, is looking for a pianist. You have been recommended for the position. You will be auditioning today." Today? I looked down at my hands. My fingernails were ragged, and my fingers were stiff. I hadn't practiced for months. I hadn't done my exercises or scales or drills.

The *Lagerführerin* looked us up and down. "You'll shower, of course. The commandant can't abide filth, so be sure to scrub your faces and clean your nails." She clicked her fingers, and the guards rushed to distribute bags. "Leave your clothes in the bags. You'll get a new dress after you shower." Her voice was clipped. "You won't get to keep it." A guard stepped forward holding a sealed cardboard box. The *Lagerführerin* pulled a switchblade from her belt, sliced the box open, then beckoned us forward to pull out a soap and shampoo. As we filed past, she assigned each of us a number. I was the last to arrive, so I'd be the last to audition.

We undressed. I shoved my dress and my cup into the bag, hoping it would still be there when I returned from the audition. Rivka stood next to me, naked and shivering. The girl beside her stood with her legs crossed and her arms folded across her chest, her face beet-red. I'd stopped blushing long ago. The washroom guards didn't see us—we were invisible to them. Invisible to God, too, it seemed. We all looked alike, anyway: flat-chested and bone-thin. Six birdlike creatures with spindly legs and sticking-out hips. The *Lagerführerin* gave the order, and we stepped into the showers. I adjusted the temperature, stuck my head under the showerhead, and let the hot water pound my face, slide down my body, swirl around my ankles, and escape down the drain.

"Grab a dress," an angry voice said from across the room. I stepped from the shower and saw Oberaufseherin Trommler standing in the *Lagerführerin*'s place. She was second in command at the camp and was rumored to be the meaner of the two women. People whispered that she kept half-starved dogs that she liked to unleash on the inmates. She had a whip in her hand and a pistol on her belt. She pointed to a rack of dresses that had been rolled into the room. "Now that the *Lagerführerin*'s gone, I'm in charge," she said, glancing down at her gun. "There's underwear, slips, brassieres, and stockings on the bench. *Schnell!*"

We dressed hurriedly under her venomous gaze. I pulled on a pair of underpants, glad that my period still hadn't come. I was a week overdue and thankful for the reprieve. Last month I'd had to work with soiled rags between my legs and sneak to the washroom to rinse them out after dark. The Polish girls hated those of us who still bled — we were considered the spoiled new arrivals because our bodies still worked.

Trommler walked among us as we dressed, handing out scarves, rouge, and lipstick. She dropped a compact of shimmering blue eye shadow on my lap and told me to tart myself up. I brushed the pressed powder lightly over my lids and skimmed the lipstick over my lips, but I didn't use the rouge. I wasn't going to pretty myself up for anyone, especially the commandant. I didn't want him noticing my lashes or admiring my lips. It was bad enough having to entertain him.

Rivka picked up a lipstick from the bench and sighed.

"I don't know how to do this," she whispered, dabbing the color on her lips.

"You need more," I whispered, pointing to her lips, but she misunderstood and grabbed the rouge. It didn't matter. It wasn't a beauty contest; it was a piano audition, and Rivka was sure to win, with or without face paint. I grabbed a pair of shoes from a box, wrapped a silk scarf over my corn-colored spikes, and followed Trommler out of the shower block.

We filed through the main gate, accompanied by two men with machine guns. It was Sunday. On Sundays the quarry was closed. Cleaning the latrines and washing down the barracks didn't warrant musical accompaniment, so on Sundays the band didn't play at the gate. We marched to our own beat—six musicians without instruments.

I was surprised to find, a few miles from our own camp, another just like it, with chimneys spilling smoke and a concrete compound of barracks. In front of the camp's main gate was a sign that read ARBEIT MACHT FREI—"Work Brings Freedom." A group of men in striped suits were repairing a barbed-wire fence. Michael Wollner was among them, but I didn't call out to him—there was a gun at my back and one at his.

The smell of the camp gave way to the smell of freshly turned soil as we neared a field. In Birkenau there was only gray—mud, concrete, and smoke. Beyond the barbed wire and only a short hike from our camp, was green, blue, and yellow—a blue sky unsullied by smog, green grass, and up ahead, a globe flower, the color of the sun, pushing through the soil. It was the first beautiful thing I'd seen in months.

We walked on, past peasants tilling the fields and farmers tending their cattle. An old man with a bent back pulled a potato from the ground and dusted it off. He looked up as we passed, saw the guns at our backs, and our stick-thin legs, and returned to his plowing. A young boy worked beside him, his gaze fixed on the ground. The girl who'd blushed in the showers turned beet-red again. I was too hungry to care what the farmers thought of us. I saw the old man drop the potato into his basket and wondered what he and the other farmers would be having for lunch.

When the green fields turned to cobblestoned streets, Trommler tucked her gun under her coat.

"I can still shoot through the fabric," she warned, "so don't do anything stupid."

The sign we'd just passed read OSWEICIM, POPULATION 12,000, but there were only a handful of people on the streets, most of them elderly. The shop windows were bare, and the townsfolk went about their business. No one stopped to watch us pass. We were just six women wearing silk scarves. We were a little thin, but we weren't doing badly; we had silk stockings and shiny shoes.

Trommler pulled out her gun when we reached the commandant's villa. The house was as big as our barrack, but it wasn't a windowless shed. It was a two-story redbrick mansion with a pitched roof and a weeping willow in the front yard. The grass was a perfect rectangle of green. Even the flowers stood at attention in their beds. The path to the front door was swept of leaves, and on the front porch were two wicker baskets, each containing a pair of black boots, beside them a scrubbing brush and a neatly folded rag. Mother would like this house.

"Shoes off," Trommler ordered, pulling her boots from her feet. I yanked off my shoes and looked down at my ragged toenails and the sores on my feet from working in shoes two sizes too small.

"Come in." The girl at the door wore a maid's outfit, a pale gray dress with a white scallop-edged apron tied at the waist. We followed her into a wide hallway. I stood under the soaring ceiling, feeling dwarfed by the towering walls. The floors were dark wood, the walls a stark, bright white, all of them bare. There were no rugs to soften the floor, no wall hangings or side tables or umbrellas in stands, no hooks on the walls on which to hang coats or keys. The commandant may have slept in this house, but it wasn't a home.

I peered down the hallway. The doors were all closed, save the very last one.

"The piano room," the girl announced, stepping aside to let us through. I followed Trommler into another vast space, but this one was softened by rugs. In the middle of the room was a Bösendorfer grand. I sat at the back of the room, my eyes glued to the glossy black piano. Tucked under the gleaming piano was a black lacquered stool with a black leather seat, and on top of the piano's polished lid sat an antique glass lamp and a handsome mahogany clock. A row of dining-room chairs was fanned out behind the piano. Lagerführerin Holzman sat at the end of the row, her blond hair in a braid, her face turned toward the window. Behind her stood a soldier with a gun slung over his shoulder, and to his left, Hitler watched from a photo in a silver frame.

A man entered the room, trailed by a German shepherd and an SS guard. He had the bearing of a man accustomed to walking through doorways first. It wasn't his height, though he was tall, or the gun gleaming on his belt, or even his uniform, which was cinched at the waist and dripping with medals. It was the way he moved across the room; he expected to be noticed.

Lagerführerin Holzman and Oberaufseherin Trommler jumped to their feet.

"Would Captain Jager like to hear some music?" the *Lagerführerin* asked. The commandant ran a hand through his cropped yellow hair, undid the top button of his jacket, and sat down. A scar ran across his square jaw, pale white against his pink skin. His eyes were a metallic blue, his smile glacial. His face gave away nothing. I'd hoped his appearance might give me some clue as to his taste in music, some hint that he preferred Hayden to Handel or romantic waltzes to fugues.

The commandant pulled a metal stick from under his chair.

"*Danke schön,* Frau Lagerführerin. Please begin."

The *Lagerführerin* called the first girl. "A10512. Take a seat at the piano."

Trommler elbowed the first girl from her seat. She scrambled to the piano, ovals of sweat under her arms. The commandant yawned before she reached the end of the first page.

"Tyrolean marches aren't to my taste," he said, ordering the girl back to her seat. The commandant wasn't a patient man. When the second girl faltered in the third stanza of Mephisto Waltz no.1, he had her wait outside. The third girl to audition played a Korngold piano sonata. My heart dipped as soon she started to play. Piri had taught me the same sonata in the ghetto, on the condition I play it whisper-quiet. I hadn't asked why; I knew Korngold was Jewish and all his sonatas were banned. The poor girl's fingers struck the keys, and I said nothing. And then the commandant was getting out of his seat, and it was too late to warn her because he was standing over her and yanking her from her seat and striking her flushed face with the back of his hand. A bruise flowered on her left cheek, and something inside me turned black. A soldier hurried to the commandant's side. He pulled his gun from his holster, thrust it at the girl's head, and forced her through the door. I cowered in my seat and watched them leave.

Commandant Jager returned to his seat and waited for his next victim. The room was silent except for the dog's heavy panting. Trommler shoved the next girl from her seat, and she sat down at the piano, her face a dangerous plum color. The commandant sat through Brahms's Scherzo in E-flat Minor and let her play a Chopin prelude through to the end, though she played it dully. She returned to her seat, trembling with relief, and Rivka took her place. She played Beethoven and Wagner, Chopin and Brahms, and she played sublimely, but that only made my heart hammer harder in my chest. The commandant lifted his hand from the scruff of his dog's neck to applaud but then thought better of it and returned to scratching the dog's head.

I walked to the piano, sick to my stomach. What if halfway through my Bach prelude my memory failed? What if the commandant detested Bach?

"Who's this one?" the commandant asked. He hadn't asked about the others.

"A10573, Herr Captain."

"Her name?"

Lagerführerin Holzman looked confused. It wasn't her job to know our names.

The commandant stared at me.

"Take your scarf off." He looked at the others. "All of you. Scarves off!"

That's when I saw him: a boy of sixteen or seventeen. It was difficult to tell his age. I'd become accustomed to boys with sagging mouths and bent backs who looked like old men. He looked nothing like the boys behind the electrified fences. His hair was the color of honey and his eyes the color of the sky. He was tanned and tall—at least a head taller than me—though I couldn't be sure because his head was buried in a book and he sat slouched in a chair. He was the second lovely thing I'd seen that day, and I wanted to strangle him. How dare he read while we play for our lives.

"You're a Jew?" The commandant's voice echoed across the room.

I turned from the boy to answer the commandant's question. "Yes."

"Where from?"

"Debrecen, Hungary." I looked across at the boy, who was stifling a yawn.

"And your position? Whom did you play for? The Budapest Philharmonic?"

I shook my head.

"The ballet?"

I shook it again. The commandant frowned and turned to Lagerführerin Holzman.

"So, what's she here for, her looks?"

"Nein," I answered in my best German. "I'm here because I play piano. I'm here because I'm good." I wasn't going to win the audition, no matter how well I played. I was no match for Rivka Hermann, but I wanted the chance to compete. I wanted to play on the commandant's Bösendorfer grand. I wanted the boy to put down his book. "I was promised a place at the Budapest Conservatorium. I was awarded the Budapest Medallion for most promising pianist under sixteen. I was the one voted most likely to—"

"You have five minutes," he said, cutting me off. "Impress me."

I climbed onto the stool and slipped my bare feet onto the pedals. I didn't know the commandant's favorite composer, but I knew this place, this piano. I knew what the commandant wanted. He wanted what we all wanted: to be transported. I didn't know where he wanted to go, but I knew where I wanted to be, so I played the music that would take me home. I played Clara Schumann's "Die gute Nacht," and when he instructed me to continue, I played a Bach sinfonia for Mother and Chopin's Waltz in A Minor for Father.

I played Liszt's Hungarian Rhapsody no. 6 for Piri and Ravel's *Gaspard de la Nuit* for Erika. I wasn't in the camps, and I wasn't playing for an extra crust of bread. I was back in my world: Hanna at the piano, in control of the harmony and the happy ending.

I looked up. The boy's nose was still buried in his book.

"Continue," the commandant said, and I lowered my head. I was deciding between *The Blue Danube* and Mozart's Piano Sonata no. 11 when something in the piano's gleaming black lid caught my eye. I hadn't seen my reflection in months, and it took me by surprise—the dull skin, the bristles, the face staring back at me. I was ugly, a skeleton in stage makeup. I saw it in the piano's mirrored surface and in the boy's refusal to look at me.

I put my hands on the keys and tried to find my way back home, but my heart wasn't in it. I delivered an empty Mozart sonata, sure that my finale had extinguished any chance I might have had for that extra crust of bread.

"Gut." The commandant unfolded his legs, took a handkerchief from his pocket, and dabbed his eyes.

We were told to line up. I smiled at Rivka. Her red hair was growing back in uneven tufts. She looked like a sad clown, with her painted red cheeks and smeared lipstick. She deserved the extra crust of bread; we all did. Piri was right. There was no shame in wanting to survive. I didn't want to die. I'd hardly lived. I wanted to keep living, and I wanted to keep playing the piano.

"So, Karl, whose music most impressed you?" The commandant turned to face the boy at the back of the room. The boy lifted his eyes from his book. He looked irritated.

"None of them, Father."

The commandant smiled. "Come, now. One must stand out."

The boy—Karl—stood up and looked us over. "That one, I suppose," he said, pointing to me.

Lagerführerin Holzman looked disappointed. "A10573? The blonde?"

"Yes, A10573." The boy's mouth twisted in disgust.

The commandant smiled. "You have a good ear." He turned to face Lagerführerin Holzman.

"You heard my son." He placed his baton on the seat and reached for his dog's leash. "We'll take her."

Chapter 6

We walked back to camp in the rain—five of us, when there had once been six. I hoped the girl with the bruised cheek, the one who had played Korngold's banned sonata, had made it back to camp. I turned my face up to the gray sky, opened my mouth, and gulped at the fat, delicious raindrops. I hadn't had anything to drink since breakfast. My cotton dress clung to my body and mud sucked at my shoes, but I didn't care. The commandant had chosen me to be his pianist.

Rivka turned to me. She didn't look sad or angry. She looked relieved. "Congratulations." She mouthed the word silently.

"Think you're lucky, do you?" Trommler dug her nails into my shoulder. "I hope you're luckier than the commandant's last pianist. She was a pretty blond thing like you. Didn't do her much good. Imagine losing a finger just because you hit the wrong note."

Trommler waited for a reaction, but I refused to give her one. I didn't let my face register surprise or fear.

"So"—she released her grip and turned to face the other girls—"if you want to say anything to the *winner* of today's little competition, perhaps instead of 'congratulations,' it ought to be 'good luck.'"

Another long hour passed. We kept walking. Globe flowers shivered by the roadside. Lulled by their beauty, I bent down to pull one from the mud, my right hand curled around its dark green stalk, when I noticed one of the guards standing over me, his boot lifted off the ground, his heel hovering over my hand. My fingers froze around the flower.

"Not the hand, you idiot!" Trommler screamed. "She's Captain Jager's new pianist. That hand belongs to him now."

I looked down at my jagged nails and blistered palms. It wasn't just the hands he owned. It was all of me. I was the commandant's now. I belonged to him. I'd sold my soul for a chance to sneak into the commandant's kitchen.

I plucked the flower from the earth and kept walking.

It was dark by the time we reached the main gate. Roll call was over, and the prisoners were being marched back to their bunks. They turned their heads to watch us pass, five women in stockings and silk scarves. A haggard old man spat at us, and then someone smiled, a young girl in a wet dress with a yellow star. Her right eye was swollen shut, and her feet were bare. I'd spent the day entertaining her jailer—I didn't deserve her smile.

I was almost glad when they herded us to block 11 to change back into our old clothes. I pulled my dirty underwear on, slid my C-sharp under the fraying waistband, and slipped my dress over my head, the tin cup dangling at my waist. Erika was already in bed when I returned to the barrack.

"I hear you got the job." The block leader stepped between me and the bunk. "I hope you can keep the boss happy. You *do* know how to keep men happy?" Her breath smelled of vodka. I stepped around her and fell onto the bunk beside Erika. My sister's eyes were puffy. Her mouth sagged. I hated seeing my sister so wretched. She'd stepped off the train at Birkenau so angry, but her anger had disappeared and with it, her strength.

I handed her the yellow flower. Half the petals had fallen off and the stem was bent, but she took the flower gratefully. She lay her head on my shoulder and wrapped her arms around my waist. She didn't ask about the audition.

"What's wrong?" I lifted her face from my neck and saw that she was crying. "Where's Mother?"

Erika buried her head in her hands.

"Where's Anyu?" I pulled away from her.

"Anyu's gone." Her face caved in. "The guards at selection made us hop up and down. They took her away." Erika's face was wet from crying. "It's just us now."

"Don't talk like that!" I shook my head. "She was too sick to work in the quarry. They've probably taken her to the infirmary."

"I don't know." Erika's shoulders slumped. "I've heard things —"

I cut her off. I didn't want to know what she'd heard. "They want us scared, not dead. They need us alive so we can work." I buried my face in her dress. *What if I was wrong?* I pulled the blanket around us and closed my eyes. "We'll see Anyu again," I said, and then we were both sobbing, our grief muffled by the scratchy wool.

We stayed like that, our bodies heaving, crying soundlessly under our blanket, until the block leader called lights out and the barrack grew still. Outside, it was dark, the cold silver moon strung up in the sky. I lay in bed but I couldn't sleep. There was so much I wanted to tell my mother. I'd been so angry at her, so hateful. I wanted to tell her that I finally understood. She hadn't chosen to ignore what was going on in the camp — she hadn't chosen to ignore us — it was just all too hard: losing her home, then her husband. I wanted to tell her that I wasn't angry with her anymore. I wanted to tell her that we'd be okay, that I had a job and a plan and a way to get food. That I'd find her and feed her, and feed Erika, too. I wasn't losing her. Not yet. Not till she'd seen me graduate from the Budapest Conservatory and watched me perform at the Budapest Concert Hall and taught me to cook and watched me walk down the aisle.

I comforted myself with Clara Schumann's Piano Concerto in A Minor, rehearsing the music in my head, picturing the notes on the page, trying to lose myself in the melody. I thought of the perilous situations Clara had survived. In 1849, during the Dresden uprising, she'd walked through the city's front lines, defying a mob of armed men, to rescue her children. Anyu and Erika had looked out for me my whole life. It was my turn to take care of them. It was my turn to be strong.

I was back in block 11 the next morning. I pulled off my dress and shoved it into the bag on the bench opposite the shower stall. Erika had bitten into the stitching of my dress to make a hole for my piano key. She thought it would be safer hidden in a bag in block 11, given our block leader's fondness for stripping our beds to search for food.

I hoped so.

When I emerged from the shower, the guard on duty directed me to the other side of the room. There was a row of metal lockers against a wall, one of which had my number on it. The guard took a key from her pocket and unlocked the door. Inside the locker was a pair of shoes, a pale-pink linen dress with a yellow star fastened at the chest, a white chiffon scarf, a cardigan, underwear, a slip, stockings, and a bra. I pulled out the clothes and shoved my worn shoes and clothing bag into the locker.

"When you undress tonight, leave your clothes over there for washing." The guard pointed to a trough on the opposite wall. "You'll find a set of clean clothes in your locker tomorrow. And don't even think about trying to keep them. The clothes are only to be worn for Captain Jager, underwear included. When you're in Birkenau, you dress like everybody else."

The guard left me to finish dressing. I pulled the pink dress from the locker and when I went to undo the buttons at the back of the neck, I noticed a tiny row of neatly stitched letters inside the collar. A name:

Eva Lakatos. She was my size, probably my age — if she was still alive. I fingered the pearl buttons and the stiff white collar, and my eyes started to fill. Eva's mother must have stitched every letter by hand and starched the collar so that it would sit just right. A tear slid down my cheek, but I batted it away. Tears got you killed. I squeezed my eyes shut and pulled the dress over my head.

"Your face!" The commandant's housemaid clamped her hands over my shoulders and steered me from the front door. "Captain Jager can't see you like this!" She dragged me to a wooden outhouse at the back of the villa. "Splash your face at the sink, wash off the mud, and straighten your scarf." She handed me a towel. A cracked mirror hung from a hook on the wall. I looked at my reflection. My eyes were red, my face pale.

"Come here every morning before you report for work." She opened the cabinet above the sink and pulled out a lipstick. "Redo your makeup, fix your scarf, straighten yourself up. The commandant likes everything in his house immaculate, including his staff."

I stared into the mirror. My dress was pretty, but it gaped at the neck. I looked like a coat hanger. The last time I had looked at myself in a mirror — really looked — I'd been trying on my yellow organza dress for Erika. I'd been shocked by my reflection then, too: shocked by the curves that were made obvious by the drape of the dress, and by my breasts and hips. Erika had brushed eye shadow onto my lids and swept my hair into a loose roll. Father had whistled from the door and I'd blushed, but I'd liked the woman I had become.

I turned from the mirror and followed the girl to the house. Her name was Vera. She was from Czechoslovakia, and had been working for the commandant for a year. She spoke quickly.

"Once we're through the front door, we can't talk until we're in the kitchen. I've a lot to tell you, so listen carefully. Leave your shoes at the front door. There are shoes for you inside. Keep them clean. You won't find shoe polish in the camp, but if you save your bread, you can trade it for margarine. Margarine makes great shoe polish." I looked at her blankly. "You'll find margarine in Canada." She looked at me and sighed. "It's the warehouse barrack behind the infirmary. They call it Canada because it's the land of plenty. I'll arrange for you to get in. You'll find everything you need there — soap, toothpaste, toilet paper . . ." She looked down at my nails. "Nail clippers, too. It all costs. A potato for a toothbrush, a piece of bread for a scrap of margarine."

"Where do they get it all?" I asked, confused.

"The suitcases left at the station. They're taken to Canada. The furs and jewelry are sent to Berlin; the rest stays at Canada for the SS and the block leaders, the interpreters, the runners . . ." She touched her bony hand to my scarf. "You could trade that scarf for margarine. They might even throw in some nail clippers if it's real silk."

"But the guards will notice it's missing."

Vera smiled knowingly. "Tell them Captain Jager used it to wipe his boots."

We reached the front door, and Vera handed me a winter coat. "Winter is coming," she said. "This is yours to keep. You mustn't get sick, not when the commandant has guests to entertain."

"My block leader hinted that the commandant likes blondes. Is that why I got the job?"

Vera's smile faded. "Captain Jager likes blondes, but he doesn't like blond Jews. He'd sooner flirt with a pack of wolves than touch Jewish skin." She opened the front door.

"One last question," I whispered. "My mother was taken last night and—"

Vera shook her head and pressed a finger to her lips. "No talking in the hallway." I tiptoed in after her. Every door she pointed to was locked, every room out of bounds, except for the music room where I'd be spending all my time. Vera stopped outside the kitchen and swung the door open. Seated at a wooden table in the center of the kitchen was an old man chopping beans. His face was creased and gray. The woman at the sink peeling potatoes wore a cheerful yellow dress, but her eyes were empty. They both wore yellow stars. They whispered their hellos.

A pot of cabbage simmered on the stove. The smell reminded me of all the wasted meals I'd left on our kitchen table in Debrecen—the abandoned peas, burned potatoes, crusts of bread, the last drops of apple juice poured down the sink, the crumbs of poppy-seed cake tossed into the bin, the fat cut from meat, the flesh left on seeds.

"We're lucky to be here washing dishes instead of carting rocks, but it's no holiday," Vera said. "The scarf, the dress, the makeup—it's just for show. You won't get a three-course meal here." She glanced back at the stove. "If the commandant is home, you won't even get lunch. Don't confuse the commandant's love of music with any feeling for those who play it. If he's home, he'll expect you to be in the music room, waiting for his summons to play."

"And if he's out?"

"If he's out, you can sneak in here to look for

scraps." Her face grew hard. "But if you're caught, you'll be shot."

I swallowed hard. "Do I practice?"

"If you want to keep this job you will . . . but only when Captain Jager is away from home. Eating, using the toilet—anything that might remind him you're human—is to be done while he's out. And don't talk to him," she said, stepping into the hallway. "Unless he addresses you first. Same goes for his son, their guests, and the guards."

I followed Vera to the music room. It looked the same as it had the day of the audition except that a small table had been rolled into the center of the room. On it sat a Black Forest cake, a strudel, a pot of tea, and an assortment of handmade chocolates. Vera looked at me and shook her head.

She'd just shown me how to stand behind the piano, with my feet together and my arms by my side, when a portly couple strolled into the room. The man was laughing at something his wife was saying, his arms encircling her doughy waist.

"Viktor, Helga!" The commandant strode in, bowed to the woman, and slapped the man on the back. "How are my oldest friends? How's Berlin?"

"We haven't come here to talk about ourselves. We've come to see our dearest friend. Tell us, Hans, how are you?" The woman looked at the commandant, then at me.

"She's the pianist," the commandant said. "I'll have her play for you."

I'd always performed best in front of an audience. It was easier to play warmed by the smiles, buoyed by the audience's expectations, jolted by the extra electricity an audience provides. But not this time, not here. I wasn't onstage. There were no draped velvet curtains, no chandeliers. I was wearing a dead girl's dress, and no matter how well I played, there'd be no applause.

I rested my hands on the keys. What was it Trommler had said about the last pianist? That she'd played the wrong note? I glanced at the commandant, seated in the front row, his legs crossed, his metal baton poised in the air. My hands trembled; my head was pounding. I started to play a Chopin nocturne, tentatively at first, wary of my fingers and nervous of the notes. By the third nocturne, my breathing had returned to normal. I was in the middle of Bach's Piano Concerto in D Minor when I saw the boy standing in the doorway, his hands in his pockets, his head bowed. His father saw him, too.

"Karl, you remember Helga and Viktor. Come and say hello." The boy took a step forward and pulled out a chair. His blond hair was perfectly parted, his skin smooth, his teeth white. If he'd lifted his head, he would have been looking straight at me.

"He's turned into such a morose boy." The commandant spoke as if his son wasn't there. "He sits in his room all day or wanders around the house with his nose in a book." He winced with irritation. "I think it's the Jews. Even being in the same room as them sets him on edge. I keep telling him, you can't catch anything by looking at them; you have to touch them for that!" He grinned broadly.

He stood up and walked toward the piano, waving his baton in the air. I was playing a Brahms intermezzo, pounding at the keys to drown out the conversation, grabbing huge handfuls of notes and hurling them into the air. The commandant stopped behind me. I could feel his warm breath on my neck. I switched from Brahms to Schubert, but he still didn't move away. He hovered over me, watching me play. At the end of the impromptu, he returned to his seat, took a handkerchief from his pocket, and dabbed at his eyes. I tried not to stare.

Vera approached the commandant. She had a silver teapot in one hand and a steaming cup of black tea in the other. She held the cup out to him. "Tea, Captain Jager?"

"Tea?" he thundered, his face turning red. "Did I ask for tea?"

Vera's shoulders sloped forward. I launched into a Mozart sonata, hoping to mute the commandant's anger, but it was too late. He lifted his baton and struck Vera's hand, sending the cup and saucer crashing to the floor, where they lay splintered and steaming.

"Get out!" the commandant yelled, his anger hot and red. Vera gathered up the broken porcelain shards, mopped up the spilled tea with her apron, and escaped to the kitchen. The commandant turned to his guests.

"So sorry for the interruption. Let me make it up to you with a little Chopin." He turned to me and lifted his baton. My hands were shaking. "The Fifth Étude?"

Karl left the room as I played the opening bars, my heart thumping away beneath my dress. The commandant had requested a happy song. I didn't feel cheerful, but after a time, I felt anesthetized by the music. Buffeted from the commandant's rage, I played the rest of the repertoire, but I played mechanically. I wondered whether Captain Jager could tell the difference.

The day dragged. A fresh pot of tea was left to brew on a side table. Strudel was sliced and swept onto plates. The Black Forest cake was cut up and disappeared. The chocolates were devoured one by one. The light grew weak, and my hands grew tired. I needed the toilet.

At half past five, the commandant's guests stood to leave and a guard was summoned to escort me to the camp. As we passed the kitchen, I turned and saw Vera sitting at the worktable, her hand wrapped in rags. The commandant's son was in the kitchen, too, pacing the floor. He was talking in a low voice, his mouth tight with anger. Vera looked up as I passed, and the boy swung around. He walked toward me and shut the door.

Chapter 7

Erika was waiting for me in the barrack. She looked gaunt and exhausted. She didn't notice my new coat. "I don't have to give it back," I whispered. "We can sleep under it." Erika didn't answer. "I can hide food in the pockets." She turned and smiled, but there was a sadness in her eyes I'd never seen before and it scared me. We stood in line for dinner, and when I got my ration, I told Erika I'd eaten and slipped her my square of bread. She took it gratefully. Our bunk mates watched her enviously, hating her for her extra ration and hating me for giving it to her. No one in the camp gave food away, not unless they were getting better food—and plenty of it—elsewhere. Erika didn't seem to notice the bitter stares or hear their pointed whispering, but I did. I saw their lips form the words *slut* and *whore* and heard them guess at the sexual favors I bestowed on the commandant.

"I'm sorry," I said, but Erika didn't look up. "They don't talk to you, and it's because of me . . ." My voice trailed off.

"It doesn't matter," Erika said. But I knew it did. She pretended not to care, but with Mother gone, me at the villa, and the twins still at the infirmary, Erika was lonely. I was content with a piano for company, but Erika needed people. She needed conversation and connection as much as she needed food and rest. I could give her my coffee, sneak her my crusts, and hold her at night, but it wasn't enough.

Vera was on the front porch shining the commandant's boots when I arrived at the villa the next day. She placed one gleaming leather boot by the door and picked up the other. Mud spattered the sides of the boot. Vera grimaced and pulled what looked like a clump of hair from the heel.

I swapped my grimy boots for clean shoes and followed Vera inside. I could hear the commandant's son talking from behind the closed door of the dining room. Vera stopped outside the door and put a finger to her lips.

"Studying by correspondence is not the same as going to school in Berlin, Father. I want to go back." *That makes two of us,* I thought, pressing my ear to the wood. I knew how it felt to want to rewind time, to want to go home, but it didn't make me feel any sympathy for Karl.

"There's nothing you can learn in Berlin that you can't learn here." The commandant's anger bled through the walls. "We're making history. If you bothered to accompany me to the camps, you'd see that. Your schooling can wait; the führer cannot!" We leaped back at the sound of a chair being scraped across the floor. Vera grabbed me by the collar, and we flew down the hallway. I turned for the music room, dizzy with fear, and Vera ducked into the kitchen. I stood with my feet together and arms by my sides, waiting for the commandant's arrival and dreading it. I waited for hours.

I rubbed my hands together to warm them, stepped from one foot to the other to stop my legs from going numb, and ran through all of Clara Schumann's concertos in my head to pass the time. I played every crotchet and semiquaver till there was no room left in my head for hunger or exhaustion or wondering or worrying. I looked around the room. It was cold, even with the afternoon sun filtering through the drapes. There was a rug on the floor, silver candlesticks on the mantelpiece, and a crystal wine decanter on the side table, but there were no family photos, no artwork or flowers. I thought of our living room in Debrecen and the photo of my parents' wedding that hung in a gilt frame on the wall, the photos of Erika and me that crowded the mantelpiece, the bundled birthday cards, travel mementos, and graduation photos that filled the bookshelves. Even when the gas in the ghetto was turned off, I'd felt warm in that room.

The commandant finally entered, trailed by his son and a man in uniform. I sat down and waited for his signal.

"I always prefer to start with a little music. Shall we listen first and talk later?" The commandant invited his guest to sit down. I played Schubert while the commandant and his guest drank a glass of schnapps.

I looked at the commandant, seated in the front row and spotlit by the sun, and then at Karl, at the back of the room, cast in shadow. That was the one difference between father and son — the commandant wore his hatred like a badge. Occasionally, he took it off when listening to music or patting Lottie, his German shepherd. Karl's anger was more muted, but it never let up. His father was quizzing his guest about the efficiency of the showers, and even that banal conversation was enough to set a muscle working angrily in Karl's jaw.

Karl turned his chair away from the piano. I knew it was rude to stare, probably dangerous, too, but I couldn't look away from him. I'd never seen anyone so still simmer with so much rage. I envied him his anger. I was angry, too — angrier than I'd ever been — but I had to bury my feelings. I couldn't scream or stamp my feet. I wasn't even allowed to cry — not here, not in the barracks, not even in the empty fields outside Birkenau. There was always someone with a gun at my back.

The commandant called for a bottle of wine, and Karl stood to leave.

"Not so fast," Captain Jager called after his son. The commandant turned to his guest. "Did you know that my son sings? At least that's what he tells me. He hardly ever sings for me, but he's happy to let me pay for his lessons." The commandant swooped on his son. "Karl, Herr Lang is in the mood for a song. Tell the girl what to play."

Karl sighed and made his way to the piano, hands deep in his pockets, his mouth drawn.

"Do you know *Die Feen*? It's Wagner." Karl pulled the sheet music from a drawer and set it down in front of me.

I nodded, unsure whether I'd heard him correctly. Wagner was one of Hitler's favorite composers, so a predictable choice. But *Die Feen* was a romantic opera, a fantasy about a beautiful fairy who renounces her immortality to spend her life with a mortal. It was a love story.

Karl stood over me. He smelled clean. I lifted my fingers to the keys and began to play. I could feel my heart pulsing under my skin. Would I be blamed if his timing was off? Was I to mask his imperfections? What if he improvised? I wanted to crawl into the piano and close the lid. I played the chords and tried to lose myself in the music, tried to hide inside it, but Karl's sloping shoulders cast a shadow over the piano and I couldn't get out from under it.

"'Gentle fairy,'" he began, his voice a burnished baritone, like melted chocolate, dark gold and rich. I was glad I hadn't been asked to sing the part of the fairy to his grieving prince. I was struggling to hit the right notes. My heart was banging away beneath my blouse, and my hands were shaking. I'd never heard a voice so full of yearning, a voice quite as beautiful, or puzzling. How could Karl have so much hate inside him, yet sing so convincingly of love? How could a boy without a heart sing of heartbreak?

It wasn't until the end of the aria that I allowed myself to look at him. Karl's eyes were empty, his mouth drawn.

The commandant sat with his hands in his lap and glanced at his son. "It's good to know the lessons weren't a complete waste of money." He called for Vera. "My guest and I will be going out for lunch." He smiled at Herr Lang. "I know you like home-cooked meals. We were going to have goulash, but I wasn't satisfied with the cut of beef — too much fat." The commandant looked at Vera. "You can take the meat. We won't be eating it." Vera's eyes widened. "Give it to Lottie. Feed her outside, then bathe her." Vera's shoulders slumped. She took the leash and led Lottie from the room.

Karl watched her leave, his hands curled into a fist, his jaw tight. The commandant left, and his guest hurried after him. Karl pulled the sheet music from the piano, put it back in the drawer, and stalked from the room.

I sat down to practice, relieved to be alone. Piri had told me once that accompanying a vocalist on the piano was like taking a lover. You had to move as one, mirror each other's moods, sense each other's fears, take one another's hand, and leap into the music.

I had leaped in alone. It was only when I stopped hammering at the keys that the gnawing in my belly returned. The house was still. I snuck from the music room and crept to the kitchen, hoping to find some leftovers from lunch, but the table was empty and the workbenches cleared. Ivanka, the cook, was wiping down the sink. Mr. Zielinski, the kitchen hand, was sweeping the crumbs from the floor. I was too proud to beg for floor scraps, but had he offered them to me, I would've picked through the dust to find a potato peel.

Vera didn't see me come in. She was at the back door, holding a wicker basket, talking to a man in a striped prison uniform. She leaned in to him, whispered something in his ear, and tipped the contents of her basket into his drawstring bag.

"Who's that?"

Vera swung around at the sound of my voice. "Just the laundry man." She rushed to close the door. "He comes from Birkenau every afternoon around three to collect Captain Jager's dirty linen." The door swung open again and an elderly man wearing gum boots shuffled in, lugging a basket of vegetables.

"You must be the new pianist." The man extended his hand. "I'm Stanislaw, the gardener," he whispered. "And you're . . ."

I looked up from his basket. "Hungry."

He tiptoed to the door and peered into the hallway, then pulled a carrot from his basket and handed it to me. I didn't peel the carrot or wash it or put it in my pocket. I shoved it into my mouth.

"I thought you were supposed to cut the leaves off

before you ate it," Vera whispered, grabbing a carrot from the basket and stuffing it into her mouth.

I wiped my mouth and smiled at Vera, at her bulging cheeks and the fleck of orange spit at the sides of her mouth and the leaf tickling her lips. But she wasn't smiling back at me: she'd turned to face the door, her hand flying up to cover her mouth. Karl stood in the doorway, staring in at her. I looked down at my feet, bit my lip, and tasted blood.

Vera had said the penalty for stealing food was a bullet to the head. I stared down at my feet. I could feel Karl watching me, but I didn't look up; I didn't move. No one did. From the corner of my eye, I could see his black leather boots. I watched them move across the room and saw them stop at the sink. I heard a cupboard door swing open, the clink of a glass, water running. No one spoke. I closed my eyes. *It was all my fault. Karl would tell his father about Vera, and the commandant would* . . . I heard footsteps retreating and looked up. Karl was gone, and Vera was wiping her mouth with the back of her hand. She straightened her head scarf and stepped into the hallway. The rest of us stood there mute, too scared to leave the kitchen, too frightened to speak.

Vera came back a few minutes later, trailed by a guard.

"Vera!" I stepped forward, my arms flung out. "I'm so sorry—" She cut me short.

"The guard's here for you," she said, and I stumbled backward. "It's almost dark. He'll walk you home."

I didn't tell Erika about the carrots, or about Karl. I stood in line for my crust of bread, inching my way to the front. I shouldn't have taken the carrot. I should have been thinking of Erika; I was responsible for her now.

The block leader held out a piece of bread and smiled. It was a big piece, no mold. I reached for it, but before I could grab the slice, she snatched it away.

"Do you think I haven't heard what you're doing?" Her smile fell away. "I'm not stupid. I know you're not going to eat this." She held up the stump of bread. "You're going to give it to your sister." The women fell silent. "Well, not anymore you're not." She flung it on the ground. A dozen women dove at her feet, clawing at the floor for the scrap of bread.

"You think you're smart, don't you?" The block leader fingered the buttons of my new coat, her hands hovering inches from the secret pocket I'd sewn into the lining late last night.

"You think that just because you work for the commandant, you're untouchable." She marched up to Erika and shoved her whip under her chin. "Well, maybe *you* are . . ." She looked back at me. "But your sister's not." And then she leaned over my sister and spat in her face.

I wanted to spit right back at her. I wanted to suck up all the hunger and hate and spit it right in her eye. I wanted to grab the bread bin and bring it down on her skull. Erika was staring at me, her face covered in spit, her eyes pleading. It was the same look I'd given her a thousand times. *Please, whatever you're thinking about doing, don't do it.* I stepped away, hating the block leader for abusing my sister and hating myself for letting her.

The block leader ran the back of her hand across her mouth. "If you give her your dinner again, I'll make sure she doesn't eat for a week."

Chapter 8

"Vera, you're here! I was so worried." I sat down on the front porch and unlaced my boots. Vera looked at me blankly.

"Where else would I be?" She put down the commandant's boots and her rag and opened the front door. I followed her into the kitchen. Ivanka was at the sink, scouring the remains of a scrambled egg from a frying pan. Mr. Zielinski was at the workbench, rolling out pastry, and Stanislaw was in the garden, tending the vegetable patch. Everybody going about their business. No one missing. No black eyes.

Karl hadn't told his father about last night.

There was a knock at the front door. I fled to the music room, and Vera ushered in the commandant's guest—a small middle-aged man with a shock of silver hair.

The commandant swept into the room a few minutes later, trailed by his son.

"*Heil Hitler!*" The little man leaped to his feet and raised his right arm.

"*Heil Hitler!*" The commandant mirrored the salute. Karl sank into a chair. He always chose the same spot, far away from the piano. I knew it wasn't the music that drove him away. He studied singing; he liked music. It was me. I didn't take it personally. It wasn't Hanna Mendel he despised; I was invisible, irrelevant. It was the Jew at the piano.

I'm not ashamed of who I am, I wanted to say. *I'm proud to be a Jew. I live behind the barbed wire with philosophers, scientists, artists, and teachers, with gypsies, poets, and composers. You live in a home filled with hate.*

"Sit up and stop frowning!" The commandant swung his baton at the legs of Karl's chair. I launched into a Beethoven bagatelle with trembling fingers. The commandant withdrew his baton and turned his attention to his guest. Karl slouched in his seat and closed his eyes, but he wasn't dozing. He was tapping his foot in time to the music. He was listening to me play.

Vera offered the commandant's guest a chocolate. He took two.

"I know I shouldn't—being a dentist—but I can't resist. Besides," he said, grinning at the commandant, "if my teeth fall out, I know where to get a false set."

He extracted a small glass jar from his briefcase and passed it to the commandant.

I looked down at the keys, but not before I'd seen what was inside the jar: teeth. *Teeth.* Yellow tobacco-stained teeth, and creamy white baby teeth, the color of the piano keys. The dentist plunged his hands back into his bag and pulled out a gold bar.

"Beautiful, isn't it?"

I battered the keys. *Beautiful?* I closed my eyes and tried to slip inside the music, but I couldn't get in. I squeezed my eyes shut, but it was still there, an image flickering against the backs of my eyelids: a man with silver hair bent over a dead body, prying open lips and pulling at gold teeth. I opened my eyes and stared at the sheet music. *Let me in,* I begged, belting at the keys, but no matter how hard I tried, I couldn't force my way in. I stared at the notes dancing across the page and felt sick. *If you feel nauseous,* Father used to say, *pick a spot in the distance and stare at it.*

I looked past the piano and the first row of chairs and saw Karl. He'd stopped dozing and was doodling on a napkin, oblivious to the exchange between his father and the dentist. My nausea dissipated, replaced by — I wasn't sure what — rage, disgust, despair. All I knew was that I wanted to tear the napkin from Karl's hands, drag him to the table, and force him to look

108

into the jar until that cold, hard face of his registered something other than indifference. I'd misjudged him. Karl didn't hate Jews. He just didn't care. That's why he didn't bother raising his head to look at the jar, and that's why he hadn't told his father about the stolen carrot. The war, our imprisonment, his father's role in the camps—none of it mattered to him. The only thing that mattered to Karl Jager was Karl Jager.

The commandant passed the gold ingot back to his guest.

"Nice watch." The dentist looked up from the commandant's wrist. "Pink gold, eighteen carat, a Jaeger-LeCoultre if I'm not mistaken?"

"Yes, given to me by my father." The commandant looked down at his watch. "I don't know why I still wear it. It doesn't keep the time like it used to."

"Then you must give it to me." The dentist held out his hand. "I'll have it fixed. There's a workshop in the camp—one fellow in particular with a knack for repairs. He restored my old pocket watch just last month."

A watchmaker with a knack for repairs? Does he wear glasses? Does he have a scar on his chin? I pictured my father bent over a workbench, surrounded by broken watches and an arsenal of spare parts.

Someone coughed. Startled, I looked up. The

dentist was staring at me. So was the commandant. I looked down at my hands. They were frozen over the piano. I'd stopped playing. I'd cut short Beethoven's bagatelle! The commandant unfolded himself from his chair, raised his baton, and took a step toward me.

"Herr Jager. It's Lottie." Stanislaw rushed into the room. "I think she's choking." The commandant's baton clattered to the floor, and he ran from the room. The dentist excused himself, pocketing a chocolate as he left, and then it was just Karl and me. My heart slammed against my chest. I'd just escaped a beating by the commandant, and there was Karl, two rows back, his father's baton on the floor in front of him. He only had to reach out and wrap his fingers around it . . .

Karl stood up slowly. He stepped away from his chair, turned for the door, and walked out of the room without a backward glance. No one came for a long time. I stood in the corner, feet together, arms by my sides, listening for footsteps. The house was quiet, but there was movement in the garden, a panting sound and then a muffled whimpering. I inched forward and looked out the window. Lottie lay on her side on the wet grass. The commandant was on his knees, bent over her, his arms wrapped around her body, his cheek pressed against her fur. Stanislaw stood behind him.

Eventually, the commandant rose to his feet and turned to the gardener. "Dig her a grave under the plum tree." He looked back at the dog. "She'd like that." He disappeared from view. I heard a door swing open, then click shut. A car started.

I returned to my corner. Later that afternoon, at the sound of the commandant's voice, I crept to the window. Captain Jager was standing at the edge of Lottie's grave, staring at the sad mound of dirt. He motioned for the gardener to approach. Stanislaw had a bunch of red poppies in his hand. He stepped onto the grave and laid the flowers on the heaped soil.

"*Verschwinde! Verschwinde!*" the commandant yelled at Stanislaw. "Get off the grave!" The commandant rammed the old man with both hands, sending the gardener tumbling backward onto the grass. Stanislaw's head hit the dirt with a thud. I stepped back from the window. I didn't want to see any more.

"You imbecile . . ." The commandant's anger seeped through the walls. Stanislaw mumbled Lottie's name. He asked the commandant to forgive his mistake, and then everything went quiet and I heard Captain Jager say, "A mistake?" He said it twice and then he said something else. He said, "Well, so is this."

I rammed my hands over my ears, but I still heard the gunshot. The sound leaked through my fingers. I bent my head and cried into my hands.

I cried for a long time, half hoping the commandant would find me in tears and order me back to camp. I didn't want to share my music with the commandant or his son, and I was sick of pretending that I did. I'd always played the piano, if not brilliantly, then at least with integrity. Now I lied every time I sat down.

I mopped the tears from my face and wiped my nose on my sleeve. I needed this job. Erika needed food, and this was the only place I could get it.

The commandant's clock chimed the hour. It was five o'clock. I walked down the hall, pulled my new winter coat from its peg on the wall, and slipped my arms through the sleeves. The moon glowed in the darkening sky. In a few moments, a guard would come to take me back to camp. I peeked into the kitchen. Ivanka was stuffing a cabbage leaf into her mouth.

"The commandant's out," she whispered, grabbing another leaf. I walked into the room and grabbed a cabbage leaf from the colander. To hell with it. Stanislaw was dead. I might've been, too, if Lottie hadn't choked when she did. No one was safe here. It didn't matter whether you played by the rules and kept your head down; you could still be shot. I wasn't safe, no matter what I did.

I stuffed the cabbage leaf into my secret pocket. A pot of water simmered on the stove. I plunged my hand into the hot stock, pulled out a handful of diced vegetables, and slipped them into my pocket.

"I thought you didn't break the rules." I looked up at the sound of Vera's voice. She was staring at my coat pocket.

"I know we're not meant to take food from the house but . . ." I swallowed hard.

Vera shook her head. "I didn't say don't steal. I said don't get caught." She reached for the rubbish bin and headed for the door.

"Can I take the rubbish out tonight?" I asked, stepping toward her, eyeing a potato peel poking from the bin. Vera looked down at the bin, saw the peel, hesitated, then handed me the bin. "Sure. We can take turns."

I walked outside, plucking the peel from the bin, when something caught my eye. It was Karl's napkin, crushed into a ball. It was the one he'd scribbled on earlier in the day. I shoved the peel into my pocket, put the bin down, and pulled out the napkin. Karl hadn't been scribbling. He'd drawn a piano on the napkin, a baby grand with a shiny black lid and black and white keys. There was a stool tucked under the piano and a butterfly hovering above it, its wings delicately veined in black ink. And then over it all, piercing the butterfly's wings and tearing at the soft leather of the stool, was a length of barbed wire. Karl had etched the spikes onto the napkin with such force that he'd torn through the cloth.

I stuffed the napkin into my pocket and ran back to the kitchen, skidding to a stop when I walked through the door. Mr. Zielinski was at the workbench, peeling a carrot, and Karl was standing over him.

"I — I was just putting out the rubbish," I stammered, though no one had asked. Mr. Zielinski passed Karl a carrot. Karl didn't look up. I don't know why I thought he would, why I imagined there was some part of him that wasn't completely anesthetized. So he sang and he could draw. That didn't mean he had a heart.

Chapter 9

"We're going to make it home, Erika. We're going to see Papa again. I heard someone talking about him at the villa. Papa's alive! He has a job fixing watches."

Erika smiled weakly. I pulled a cabbage leaf from my pocket and pressed it into her palm. It wasn't the most elegant dining room, but the latrine block at Birkenau was the safest place to share my spoils, so we sat on the ground and swatted flies and ate cold diced carrots and potato peels. I passed Erika a beet peel. "Keep it for the next selection," I whispered. "Rub it on your cheeks to redden them." Erika nodded. We'd seen women pinch their cheeks before presenting themselves for inspection, but the healthy flush soon drained from their faces. Beet juice would work better.

"I've never stolen before," I told my sister, feeling ashamed and proud at the same time.

"I know." Erika squeezed my hand. "Thank you."

I looked at my sister's narrow shoulders and bony kneecaps. She was the size of a ten-year-old.

"Remember what you said to me, Erika, back at the brickyard? You said that you'd do whatever it takes to get us back to Debrecen."

I wondered whether my sister had even heard me.

"I know," she said finally, her voice bleak. "I've let you down. I'm sorry."

"No, that's not what I meant." I grabbed her hand. "What I was trying to say was that it's time I grew up and took care of myself." The last thing I wanted to do was make Erika feel guilty. She hated not being able to play the protective big sister. I'd seen it on her face when I'd pulled the cabbage leaf from my pocket. I saw it every time I helped her out of bed. I looked into her big, sad eyes. "I'm almost sixteen, Erika. I'm not a kid anymore." I pressed the last scraps into her palm and stood to leave. "There's something I have to do. You stay here and finish eating."

Since I'd arrived at Birkenau, I'd been careful to avoid the block leader, so she was surprised, and a little suspicious, when I approached her in the barrack.

"What do you want?" She narrowed her eyes.

"I don't want anything," I said. "I'm here to give you something."

"And what might that be?" She grabbed my arm and walked me to the front door, away from prying eyes.

"A little token of my appreciation," I whispered, passing her a cabbage leaf.

"You're not as dumb as you look." She plunged the vegetable into her pocket. "I hope you don't think this will buy you any favors."

"Favors?" I acted offended. "No, of course not. It's only that, now that my mother is gone, I guess you're the only one who's looking out for me, looking out for all of us. Anyway, I just wanted to say there's more where that came from, and thank you."

The block leader nodded. She didn't want me to think that she could be bought, but we both knew how it worked. If I gave her an apple, she'd make sure I made it back to the commandant's villa the next day so I could steal another. And if Erika gave her a turnip or a beet, she'd look out for my sister, too.

Erika was frail, and over the next weeks, she only grew frailer. I wished I could take better care of her. I fed her scraps from the commandant's table, but she still had to march to work and haul stones and dig up earth. She had to stand bare-legged at roll call in a thin cotton dress while I waited beside her, warm in my long winter coat. She had to stand naked at selection, while I sat inside and waited. If it was raining, she stayed wet all day. I spent my days sitting on a leather stool in stockinged feet in front of a fire. Erika knew all this, and still she waited for me at the barrack door at the end of each day and pulled me close at bedtime so that we might keep each other warm.

It had been months since we'd seen our father and weeks since I'd returned from the commandant's house to find my mother gone. I still caught myself watching for my mother's shape as the women returned from the quarry at night. I missed her voice, and I missed my father's smile. I thought I saw him once—a stooped figure slowly walking up a hill—but it wasn't Papa, just a farmer with the same slight frame and curly brown hair.

Erika shared my mother's high cheekbones; I had my father's long lashes and his nose. We liked to fall asleep looking at each other. It was the only way to keep them close. There were nights I missed my parents so badly that I wanted to grab the block leader by the throat. I was sure she knew what had become of them. Instead I gave her whatever food I could scrounge. There were dozens of starving girls who needed the food more, and who were more deserving of it, but none of those skinny, hollow-eyed girls could tell me where my parents were or put in a good word for my sister if a job became available in Canada.

I'd been to the warehouse twice since learning about it from Vera. The first time was to trade my silk scarf for margarine, the second time to trade a stolen carving knife for a pair of boots for Erika. The storeroom was what I imagined heaven would look like — heaven for a prisoner: tables laden with bread, jam, sugar, and chocolate, and shelves lined with shampoo, soap, perfume, and combs. Slippers and brassieres lay in neat piles on the floor, and girls with colored kerchiefs and gray smocks wandered the aisles. Hundreds of workers kept the storeroom shelves stocked, and still the women couldn't keep up with the stream of goods flowing through the doors.

Autumn made way for winter, and the cold Polish sun disappeared behind clouds. Outside the music-room window, only a few leaves of deep red clung to the plum tree. Everything was tinted gray: the fog, the thick mud that clung to our shoes, our faces. Birkenau's barbed-wire fences and watchtowers tipped me toward hopelessness. There was no escaping, and no end to the war. We heard fighter planes scream overhead, and one night saw the sky red and raining down with bombs. But when dawn came, the barracks stood unharmed, and the band still played a death march. I still had to trudge to the villa, Erika still had to dig trenches, and the guards still had guns.

The Jewish New Year, Rosh Hashanah, passed without fanfare. I couldn't sing the praises of a God I no longer believed in, or wish Erika Happy New Year. When the holiest of religious days, Yom Kippur, arrived, at the end of September, I didn't fast. I swallowed my coffee defiantly and refused to ask God to forgive my sins. And when we fell into bed and a woman in the next bunk sang Avinu Malkeinu, I didn't join in. "Hear our prayer," she whispered. "*Sh'ma kolenu.* Inscribe us for blessing in the Book of Life."

It was easy to die in Birkenau: You looked a guard in the eye or stumbled from the line on the way to the washroom. I saw a girl refuse to get out of bed and another spit at a guard. They were both dragged outside and shot. I wasn't going to help death along. I stole, but I wasn't stupid. I took risks, but they were calculated. I wanted to make it out alive, so I did things I wasn't proud of. I stayed silent when other girls were beaten, and I stole from an inmate. I woke up one morning to find the girl who'd been sleeping beside me was dead, so I did what I'd seen dozens of girls do before me: I searched her pockets for a crust of bread.

I couldn't eat the handful of crumbs I found; I gave them to Erika.

In Debrecen I'd left behind a beautiful wall calendar. Each page had a scene from a famous opera and a portrait of a composer whose birthday fell on that month. I shared my December birthday with Beethoven. Clara Schumann's was in September. I'd wanted to pack the calendar, but there hadn't been room for it. In Birkenau, there was no need for it. Calendared time didn't matter in the camp. It only mattered that I made it to the commandant's home every morning, sat down at his piano, and played the right chords. Every day was the same as the day before: the commandant and his guests would have morning tea and talk over Bach, and Karl would sit sullenly in the corner. Every day was a repeat of the day before. Every day was tedious and gray until one day in November, when everything changed.

The commandant, Karl, and I were in the music room. Vera had been sent to the kitchen to make tea.

"What's taking her so long?" the commandant grumbled. "For heaven's sake, go see what the hold up is."

I ran to the kitchen, turned into the doorway, and

slumped to my knees. Vera was lying on the kitchen floor on a bed of shattered porcelain.

"Vera, what happened?" She looked like a broken doll. Limp tea leaves clung to her dress, and her scarf was slick with blood. She opened her mouth, but no sound came out. I lifted her head from the floor.

"Vera, who did this to you?" Her eyes flickered toward the window. A guard was pacing the driveway, SS standard issue — cropped blond hair, hard blue eyes, crisp gray uniform — one of a dozen faceless guards who patrolled the grounds. I turned back to Vera.

"What happened?"

"He hit me, I fell backward . . ."

"But why?"

"I couldn't . . ." She shook her head. "It doesn't matter. Hanna, I need you to do something."

"Of course, Vera. Anything." I reached up, pulled a rag from the bench, folded it, and slipped it under her head.

"I need you to . . ." Vera closed her eyes.

"What Vera? What do you need me to do?" I leaned down. I was so close, I could feel her lips brush the tip of my ear.

"I need you to take over the laundry shift. Tell Karl I said it was okay." She let out a thin cry. "It hurts."

"You're going to be okay," I said. What I wanted to

say was, *Please don't die.* And then Karl walked in. "She needs help. Please. Get some help."

"What happened?" Karl asked without looking at me.

"Yes. What happened?" the commandant echoed, stepping into the room. I looked through the window at the guard, who was now seated on a bench, his head in his hands. It was safer not to accuse anyone and let the commandant work it out.

"Klaus!" the commandant hollered, stepping outside.

"Please. She needs a doctor." I turned to Karl. He was watching his father guiding the guard back into the house.

"I'll put a phone call through to Lagerführerin Holzman." The commandant stepped over Vera as he spoke to Klaus. "She'll arrange a replacement. Let's hope she's better at making tea." He looked down at Vera, sprawled on the floor.

"Father, shouldn't she be seen to? Your physician isn't far. . . ."

The commandant looked at his son. "Dr. Huber has better things to do," he began, "but perhaps you're right." He stopped to consider his son's suggestion. "She mustn't die here. Too messy. Klaus, take her back to Birkenau." And then he stalked out.

The soldier pulled Vera to her feet and dragged her outside.

"Wait!" I called after Karl as he turned to leave. "I have a message from Vera." I held my breath. Karl swung around to face me. "She asked me to do the laundry shift. She said to tell you it was okay."

He looked past me to the window. I felt my cheeks flush. *Of course it was okay. What difference did it make to Karl who did the laundry?*

"Okay," he said. "Meet me here at three o'clock."

I'd been waiting for ten minutes, trying not to look at the spot where Vera had lain, when Karl walked into the kitchen lugging a wicker basket. He carried it to the back door and motioned for me to follow him. He set the basket down and looked out the window into the garden, his gaze suddenly intent. In the basket were sheets, towels, and tablecloths. The grandfather clock in the hallway chimed three.

"Any minute there'll be a knock at the door. Take this," he said, lifting the basket from the floor and handing it to me. It was heavy.

"It's the laundry," he explained. "Ivanka collects the dirty linen every day after lunch. She used to leave it for Vera." He lowered his voice. "From now on she'll leave it for you." He looked at me, but I couldn't read his expression. I only knew that his eyes were even bluer close-up. Blue flecked with green.

"Tibor will knock on the door at three. Give him the basket."

There was a knock at the back door, and Karl rushed from the room. I reached for the door handle. A scrawny man in a striped jacket poked his head through the door.

"Where's Vera?"

"Vera's been hurt. She's been taken back to camp. I'm Hanna. Are you Tibor?"

He nodded.

"She told me to take over her shift," I continued, holding up the basket. He opened his drawstring bag, and I tipped the laundry into it.

"She trained you well," he whispered, pulling an apple from the bag. I looked at the apple. Then I looked into the bag. Lying among the sheets and towels and pillowcases were a loaf of bread, a scattering of potatoes, and a jumble of apples.

"I didn't p-put them there," I stammered, shaking my head.

"Of course you didn't." He winked. "Take the apple." He held out his hand. "I have to go. They're waiting for me at the laundry."

"Who's waiting?"

"Andor, Vera's brother. I give him the food, and he distributes it. There are a lot of hungry people in Birkenau." He threw the bag over his shoulder and walked to the truck idling in the driveway. I scooped up the empty wicker basket and closed the kitchen door. *Tibor. Karl had told me to give the laundry to Tibor.* The basket slipped from my fingers and clattered to the floor. Karl knew the name of the man who collected his laundry. He knew what time it would be collected and the name of the girl who changed the sheets. He'd called Vera by her name, too. He could have used their numbers. He could have called Ivanka "the maid." He could have called Tibor "the Jew who did the laundry."

He'd used their names.

Chapter 10

I had so much to tell Erika. I swung the barrack door open, handed the block leader my apple, fell onto the bunk beside Erika, and burrowed into her.

"Vera's been hurt." I was going to tell Erika about Tibor and the laundry basket and my conversation with Karl, but first I needed to talk about my friend.

"How bad is she?" Erika asked, wiping the tears from my eyes.

"Bad." I looked up at her. "What's that?" I pointed to a red gash on her forehead.

"It's nothing, just a scrape. Tell me about Vera."

"I'll tell you everything, once you tell me what happened."

"I was at the quarry. I was working too slowly. One of the foremen got angry. It looks worse than it feels." Erika didn't want to talk about it. She never wanted to talk about it — about the work, her hunger, the guards, the girls. I knew she was just trying to protect me, but it felt like a punishment.

I tore a strip of silk from the lining of my coat and wrapped it around Erika's forehead. I wished I could do more. I wished I could stop them from hurting her. I reached into my pocket and pulled out a handful of green beans. Then I lifted my skirt and pulled a few small carrots from my underwear. It didn't matter that Erika hated green beans or that I'd stowed the carrots in my underpants. She thanked me for them, treating me like I was some brave hero, when really I was just a coward who deserted her every day to hide out in the commandant's villa.

"So will you do it?" Erika asked after I told her about the laundry basket. "Will you get the food to Tibor tomorrow?" Her eyes flashed. I hadn't seen that look of rebellion on my sister's face for a long time.

Vera's words echoed in my ears. *Take over the laundry shift.* She'd meant for me to see the food. And she was relying on me to have a basket ready for Tibor tomorrow. I replayed every scene in my head, every look, every conversation I'd had that day. Karl had whispered his instructions, he'd carried the heavy basket into the kitchen, he'd been expecting a knock at the door at three, and he knew our names. Did he know about the food in the laundry hamper? I thought about the love song he'd sung and the butterfly drawing. Maybe I'd been wrong about Karl. . . .

The block leader ordered us all out of our bunks.

"There's something I want you to see," she said, stroking her whip. I forced myself to look as she dragged a woman from her bunk and ordered her to stand in the middle of the hut. If we didn't look, if we turned our heads or closed our eyes, we'd be next in line. She told the woman to lift her dress and bend over. We watched and counted under our breath—one red welt across the back of the woman's legs, two, three. The woman's knees buckled when the block leader reached fifteen, but she didn't cry out. The block leader put her whip down at forty and went to bed.

"What did you do?" Frightened voices floated up from the bunks. The woman pulled her skirt down and looked at the women huddled on the bunks. Her eyes were dry.

"I stole a carrot from the kitchen."

It was drizzling when I left the barrack the next morning. I walked past women shivering in their cotton dresses, their egg-white scalps slick with rain, and the band bent over their instruments, wooden smiles on their faces. The guards stood over the work gangs with whips, their hands warm in their woolen mittens. The sky was gunmetal gray.

I was glad I hadn't told Erika about Karl. Why would a boy who had everything risk it all for a few Jews? The rest of the world wasn't interested in saving us. Why would Karl be any different? Handing me a laundry basket and knowing our first names didn't make him an ally.

By the time I sat down at the piano, I was convinced I'd imagined it all — the whispered words, the look Karl gave me when he handed me the basket.

I touched my fingers to the keys. The commandant drove his fork into a slab of cheesecake and shoveled it into his mouth. He dabbed his lips with a napkin, stood up, and walked toward me.

"What's that you're playing? That song, what's it called?"

My foot froze on the pedal. I'd been so intent on the commandant's conversation with his guest, a monocled SS colonel, that when Schumann's *Reverie* ended, I'd drifted into Mendelssohn's Adagio in F Major, a piece I knew by heart. The commandant had to know it was Mendelssohn and that Mendelssohn was a Jew and his music was forbidden. I thought of the girl who'd auditioned before me, the one who'd played Korngold and had not been seen since.

"Well? Who is it?" The commandant picked up his baton. Was this some kind of test? Should I feign ignorance or admit my error? My hands slipped from the keys. The commandant was growing impatient. The colonel leaned forward in his seat, his monocle glinting in the sun. I cleared my throat.

"It's . . ." But I couldn't go on. I hung my head and waited for the blows.

"It's one of Franz Hirsch's early compositions." I looked up. Karl was walking toward the piano. "It's a piece about the Rhineland." He looked his father in the eye.

"Franz Hirsch, you say?" The colonel looked at Karl. "Never heard of him."

"Well, that's understandable," Karl said. "He wasn't popular, except with the critics and those in the know. He was a student of Schubert. You don't hear the piece much these days. It's quite beautiful, don't you think, Father?"

The commandant looked confused.

"Of course. Franz Hirsch. It was on the tip of my tongue. A beautiful piece of music." The commandant turned to me. "Continue."

I looked over at Karl. Franz Hirsch? I'd never heard of the composer. And I was pretty sure Karl hadn't, either.

At the end of the sonata, the commandant and his guest left for a meeting. Karl stayed in the far corner of the music room, reading.

"Thank you," I whispered, but Karl didn't look up.

I took a deep breath. "Thank you." I forced the words out again, louder this time, but he still didn't look up from his book. Or say anything. He just kept reading. I don't know what I expected, but I felt cheated somehow.

I stared out the window, at the winter-white sky. Was I really so horrid that it pained him to look at me?

"Hanna."

I looked up, struck by the sound of my own name. Karl was standing in the doorway.

"You're welcome."

"Sorry?" I said, rising from the piano.

"You're welcome . . . for before. . . ." His face was a deep crimson, his voice so faint I could hardly hear him. He dug his hands into his pockets and looked at his feet.

"Who's Franz Hirsch?" I asked as casually as I could, as if it were nothing out of the ordinary, the two of us talking.

"Franz Hirsch?" he looked up as he stepped from the room. "He was my fifth-grade geography teacher."

At a quarter to three, I snuck to the kitchen. The

house was quiet. The commandant was out; Rosa, the girl who had replaced Vera, was sweeping the porch; Ivanka was upstairs; and Mr. Zielinski was in the garden doing Stanislaw's job. The laundry basket was by the back door. I lifted a towel and peered into the mess of soiled linens. No food. I bit my lip and tried to stay calm. I had fifteen minutes to fill the basket, and there was nothing on the stove and no food on the workbench. I swung around to face the pantry. What choice did I have? I'd promised Vera I'd take over her shift. I grabbed the laundry basket and dragged it into the pantry. I had to be smart. There were plenty of potatoes, so I could probably take one or two without them being missed. I lifted a sheet from the basket and tossed the potatoes in. I took three apples, a loaf of stale bread, an onion, a small square of cheese, and a handful of walnuts, tossing them one after the other into the basket, as quickly as I could. A bowl of raisins sat uncovered on a shelf. I dug my hand into the bowl and scooped a handful into my pocket and another into my mouth. Then I pulled the sheet back over the basket and slunk out of the pantry.

I ran to open the back door as soon as I heard Tibor knock.

"Is it all here?" The man looked anxious.

"Yes. Same as yesterday." I tipped the swollen load

into Tibor's drawstring bag. Something small and brown tumbled out of the basket.

"What's this?" Tibor reached into the bag and pulled out a parcel wrapped in brown paper and tied with string. "You're Hanna, right?"

"Yes."

"It's addressed to you." He dropped the parcel into my hand. "Open it."

I stood there blinking, sweat prickling my forehead. Someone had gotten to the laundry basket and hidden it under the sheets.

"It could be something important, something I need to pass on to Andor." Tibor stared down at the quivering parcel. My hands were shaking. I untied the string and pulled back the paper. Inside the wrapping was an egg, a perfectly smooth, perfectly white, perfectly plump, peeled, hard-boiled egg. I hadn't eaten an egg, hadn't seen an egg, in four months.

"I don't understand." I shook my head. Was this a trap? Should I give the egg back?

"What's to understand? You get an egg from the commandant's son, you take it, you eat it, and you don't ask questions." Tibor stared at the egg.

"The commandant's son?" I looked up, surprised. "How do you know it's from his son?"

Tibor's eyes narrowed. "Vera didn't tell you?"

"Tell me what?"

"Tell you about Karl. He's the only one here — besides you and me — who knows about the basket."

"He knows that we smuggle food into Birkenau?" I could feel the hairs on my arms rise.

"Of course he knows." Tibor hoisted the drawstring bag over his shoulder and reached for the doorknob. "It was his idea."

Chapter 11

"You'll never guess what I've got." I dragged Erika onto our bunk and pulled Karl's gift from my pocket.

"An egg?" Erika's eyes darted across the room. "Put it away before someone sees it." She forced my hand back into my pocket. "Where'd you get it?"

"You won't believe me if I tell you."

"Nothing surprises me anymore. Try me."

"It's from Karl."

"Karl?" Her voice rose an octave. "Karl, the commandant's son?"

I pressed a finger to her lips and nodded.

"You're right: I don't believe you."

"Maybe I was wrong about him."

Erika shook her head. "Why would he do that? Why would the commandant's son give you an egg?"

I looked at my sister. "I don't know."

I slipped off my coat, and we huddled under it. Erika tore the egg in half and passed me my share, swallowing hers in one gulp. I held the slippery white skin in my mouth before letting it slide down my throat. I trapped the yolk with my tongue and sucked at its sweetness until there was nothing left.

We fell asleep spooned together under my warm winter coat, the taste of sunshine on our tongues. The sky was still dark when I woke from a dream. I was at the villa at dusk with Karl. We were outside, alone, together. My hair was long. I was wearing my yellow organza dress, the one Mother made for the youth group's summer dance. Karl was wearing a blue-and-white striped shirt and a pair of gray trousers. He was watching me pick globe flowers. And then he walked over, took me in his arms, and kissed me. And then Mr. Zielinski walked into the garden and Karl spun around, but he wasn't wearing a blue and white shirt anymore; he was wearing an SS uniform. And he shot Mr. Zielinski.

I climbed out of my bunk. I needed the toilet. The night guard took my number down, gave me a bucket, and swung the door open. I shuffled out into the frozen night, the wet, warm bucket knocking against my legs. I set it down, hoisted up my dress, and crouched over it, disgusted with myself. I pictured my father, bald and bone-thin in a blue-and-white striped shirt and ill-fitting trousers, lying alone on a bunk, wondering if his daughters and wife were alive. I thought of my mother in the infirmary, losing her mind. The thought of Karl and me kissing would horrify them. It *was* horrifying. I shook my head to dislodge the dream. I didn't want to be thinking about Karl and how his arms felt around my waist, what his lips felt like, what Mr. Zielinski's torn-up face looked like. I pulled my dress down, carried the bucket back inside, and crept to my bunk. Light spilled from the window of the block leader's room at the far end of the barrack. I reached into my coat and pulled the raisins from my pocket. In my rush to get to Erika, I'd forgotten to give the block leader her nightly due.

I snuck to her room, tapped gently on the door, and pushed it open. I'd never been inside the block leader's room. It wasn't much better than ours. She had a nightstand, a small cupboard for her clothes, a single bed and a blanket, but the walls were peeling and the room was cold. The block leader was slumped in a chair. She looked up.

"What're you looking at?" She lifted a bottle to her lips.

"Nothing." I held out my hand and showed her the raisins. "They're for you. I meant to give them to you earlier." She swept the raisins from my palm. Stared at them.

"Marek loved raisins."

"Who?"

"Marek, my son." She put down the bottle. "What do you care?" Her face hardened. "Safe and warm in the commandant's house. You think he's gonna take care of you?" She threw back her head and laughed. "Know how I got here? Know how I got to own this whip?" I shook my head. I didn't want to know. "Three soldiers came to my house. It was a Friday night. I'd just lit the Sabbath candles." She picked up the bottle and took a swig. "They made us go outside and dig a ditch. I didn't know what it was for, this ditch. How could I know?" She rose from the chair and gripped the bed to steady herself. "They shot my husband first. Then they shot Marek." She sat down on the bed. "He was three." Her face caved in. "They rolled Nikolai into the ditch, then Marek. They gave me a spade. They pointed a gun at my head and made me bury them. Nikolai was still breathing."

They rewarded her for her effort. They threw her in a cattle truck with a hundred other Polish Jews, and when they arrived in Birkenau, they made her a block leader.

"They said if I was tough enough to bury a husband and child, I'd make a good barrack boss." She fell onto the bed. I took the bottle from her hand and pulled the blanket over her.

*   *   *

"What's the point of washing?" Erika complained as we walked to the washroom the next morning. "They'll still use their truncheons no matter how sweet I smell." I unwound the silk bandage from Erika's head. She'd stopped bleeding, but the gash on her forehead hadn't knitted together. It looked angry and red. I turned on a tap and helped Erika out of her dress. Her legs were like toothpicks.

"The point is to stay human, remember?" It felt like a lifetime since my sister had said those same words to me. Erika bent over the bowl of brown water and splashed her face. I pulled another scrap of silk from the lining of my coat, held it under the tap, and used the wet cloth to wipe down her arms and legs. A mob of women surrounded us, eyeing the rag. Erika pointed to a small, pale girl who'd been elbowed from the group. I pushed through the clawing group and placed the wet rag in the girl's hand.

"Thank you," she whispered, running the rag under her arms as the women descended upon her. I helped Erika into her dress, and we walked back to the barrack.

"I have to go," I said, tipping up my cup and sucking out the last drops of black water. The woman next to us pulled a crust of bread from under her blanket, shook the lice from the bread, and slipped the crust into her mouth.

I took Erika's face in my hands. "Don't give up, Erika. Don't lose hope." She looked so small and old. She climbed onto our bunk and gave me a wan smile.

"Hope's tiring."

I should've dragged her out of bed, but I was late for my shower. I ran to block 11, warmed my body under the spray, and stepped into my clothes. The rain that had tapped on the tin roofs of our huts for the last eight days continued unabated, and by the time I reached the villa, my coat was soaked through and my legs were spattered with mud. I changed my shoes and ran to the music room.

"The commandant won't be requiring you this morning." Rosa set a pot of tea on the side table and stepped into the hallway, closing the door behind her. "You can make yourself useful in the kitchen."

"What did he say?" A wave of nausea snuck up on me. "Am I in trouble?"

The girl's thin lips curled upward. "I wouldn't know." She smiled crudely. "Perhaps you can ask his son."

I reached out and grabbed her apron. "Please, what have you heard?"

"I've heard nothing. What? You think Captain Jager

spends his days talking about you?" She shook me off. "Dr. Mengele is coming over, and the commandant doesn't want us listening to their conversation — that's all."

"Dr. Mengele?" I chased her down the hall to the kitchen. In the three months since Lili and Agi's disappearance, two other sets of twins had made their beds in our barrack, then been called away by Dr. Mengele. "He's interested in twins," I said, not wanting to end the conversation. The new girl might know where Lili and Agi were or have information about my parents.

"Yes." She passed me a plate and a rag. "He calls them his children." She stared at me. "That doesn't sicken you?" she said, stepping toward me. I edged away from her. "You really have no idea, do you?"

I shook my head.

"He conducts experiments on them."

I felt like I was slipping underwater. I felt like I was drowning. I played Schumann's *Fantasie* in my head to stay afloat, to stop myself from slapping her, to stop myself from screaming.

As soon as the commandant and Dr. Mengele left the villa, I ran to the music room. I sat down at the piano and stabbed at the keys.

I played Beethoven and Bach. I played until I didn't

142

know what I was playing anymore. I played until I was inside the music, hidden between the bass line and the treble, slipping between the sounds, numbed by the notes. I played till my fingers were sore.

When I stopped playing, I saw Karl sitting in the corner. I slipped from my stool and grabbed a rag from the shelf to clean the piano. I knew I should thank him for his gift, but when I looked over at him, he shifted in his seat and brought his book up to hide his face. I slunk back to my stool. My reflection stared back at me from the black lacquered lid: shaved head, long neck, tired eyes. What was I thinking—that he'd welcome a conversation?

Sleet tapped at the windows. I stared at the keyboard, and the keyboard stared back at me.

"The war won't last forever." I looked up. Had Karl just said what I thought he'd said? I opened my mouth, closed it again. Karl put down his book. "I've heard rumors that the Russians are close."

I nodded. "I used to think about going home all the time."

"And now?"

"I don't know." The question was too intimate, but I couldn't help feeling touched that he'd asked. "Sometimes it's easier not to think about the people you miss."

"Then, just play piano. Forget everything else." Karl glanced at the door. The hallway was empty. "I've seen you do it. When you're at the piano, your eyes glaze over." His face flushed. "Sometimes you smile." He dropped his voice to a whisper. "Play something," he said, but I didn't lift my hands to the keys. *He'd been watching me.* All those times I'd thought his nose was stuck in his book, he'd been peering over the pages, watching my hands and my eyes and my lips.

"I said play! Now!"

I jumped at his anger. Then I looked behind him and saw his father.

The commandant had walked into the room and stopped behind his son.

"Father, you're back?" Karl turned to his father, feigning surprise.

"What's this?" The commandant brushed his son aside and stepped toward me. He held out a gloved hand. "It was on the kitchen floor."

My hands froze on the keys. My C-sharp lay in his palm. I must have ripped a hole in the secret pocket of my coat when I tore off some of the lining for Erika. I hung my head. The commandant leaned over the piano and brushed his hands over the keys.

"It's not one of ours," he said, walking toward me, "so where did you steal it?" He held the note as if it were a dagger. I stood there, paralyzed. Had he searched my coat? Had he found the secret pocket? He pressed the note to my throat, drove the splintered wood into my skin. "Answer me!"

"It's mine," I croaked, stumbling backward. "From home."

The commandant shook his head and turned away. "Sentimentality is dangerous." He hurled the C-sharp into the fire and stalked away. "My son has learned that lesson. You'd do well to learn it, too."

I watched the flames curl around the rectangle of wood, but I didn't let myself cry. I kept my head bowed and my face blank.

The commandant called for a guard to escort me home, then disappeared into his study. I turned to Karl. He was bent over the fire, stoking it, his face so close to the flames, his skin glowed orange. Something clattered to the floor by his feet. I turned toward the sound. On the hearth, blistered from the heat but still whole, was my black C-sharp.

Chapter 12

Karl was waiting for me in the kitchen the next day.

"I only have a moment." Karl looked nervously at the door. "Father's in the dining room." He reached into his trouser pocket and pulled out my C-sharp. I took it from him. His hand was warm, his fingers smooth.

"Thank you."

"He shouldn't have thrown it in the fire." Karl shook his head. "What he said about sentimentality, ignore him."

I wanted to ask him what he meant, but Ivanka walked into the room with a tray of breakfast dishes. She laid the tray by the sink and filled the basin with water. Karl plunged his hands into the soapy water. I reached for a dishcloth, but he shook his head.

"I told my father I had to wash my hands." Karl spoke quickly. "Better if they're wet."

All our conversations were like that—half finished, tentative. They were small offerings at first—a whispered word about a piece I was practicing or the tilt of his sketch pad toward the piano. Single words, scraps of information. From the books he left piled on the floor, I knew he loved horses. He learned about me through my music.

The winter wore on, and we grew more bold. I told Karl about my mother's disappearance. I was on the porch one morning, taking off my boots. He was heading out. We had less than a minute. I faced the door while I untied my laces. He faced the street.

"I got back from the audition, and she was gone," I whispered.

"I'm sorry," he said, but he didn't turn to look at me.

That's how it always was when we spoke. Karl facing away from me or looking past me or staring down at his feet, never looking me in the eye.

"I miss her," I whispered, my breath pale in the frozen air.

"My mother's dead," he said. "I miss her, too."

I looked forward to those moments, even though I knew I was supposed to hate Karl. He was the enemy, or at least the enemy's son. He slept under an eiderdown, read by the fire, ate when he was hungry, and rested when he was tired. I wanted to hate him.

I tried, but then he'd hide a biscuit wrapped in tissue between the sheets in the laundry basket or leave a drawing on his chair, knowing I'd see it, and my resolve would weaken.

I found myself looking forward to my days at the villa. Knowing I'd see Karl the next morning made the nights easier. I'd lie on my bunk, my joints stiff from the cold, my arms wrapped around Erika to stop her teeth from chattering, and I'd think about Karl tucked up in bed, reading, or singing an aria for his tutor, or drawing in the music room. I hated the camp, and I hated the snowflakes that clung to my hair and dripped down my back. I hated roll call and I hated the guards, but I couldn't hate Karl.

I turned sixteen in Birkenau. It was the eleventh of December, 1944. A Monday. Erika nudged me awake.

"I was going to bake you a cake." She smiled weakly. "But we're all out of flour. So I got you this." She reached under the bunk and pulled out a piece of bread. In the center of the slice was the stub of a candle burned down to the quick.

It was still dark outside, and the women on either side of us were fast asleep. I pretended to blow out the candle, and then we shared the "cake." I'd always looked forward to birthdays—to the party and the presents and growing a year older. This year I just wanted to know that Mother and Father were alive and that there was a chance we'd celebrate my seventeenth birthday together in Debrecen.

When I saw Rosa on the steps of the villa that morning, I didn't tell her it was my birthday. I'd hoped she and I might become friends, but Rosa didn't want friends.

"The commandant is out," she reported stiffly. "He's entertaining visitors from Berlin. They'll be having lunch in town. Upon their return, you're to play Wagner and Bruckner."

"No Schubert?"

She shook her head.

"Chopin?" I ventured a smile. "What about Brahms?"

Rosa rolled her eyes and walked inside.

I shook the snow from my coat and followed her into the house. The warmth was an assault after the bitterly cold hike. Rosa disappeared up the stairs with a bucket and mop. I peered into the kitchen. It was empty. So was the dining room. Maybe Karl was out with his father. I headed to the music room, hoping I was wrong, hoping he was sitting by the window with a sketch pad in his hand, but he wasn't. I stood in the corner until lunchtime, then crept to the piano to practice. I was halfway through Mozart's Piano

Concerto no. 4 when Karl walked in. His hair was slick with oil, and he wore a tie knotted at his neck. I tried to ignore how handsome he looked.

"Do we have *Tristan and Isolde*?" he asked, rifling through some sheet music. "Father wants me to sing it next week for some guests." I wondered if he knew that the name Tristan meant sorrow and that he died of a broken heart in the last aria.

I rummaged through the cupboard next to the piano.

"You do," I said, sitting down and setting the music on the piano stand.

"I don't know all the words," he said, walking around to where I sat. "Do you mind?"

He stopped beside me and leaned in to read the music.

"Of course not," I said, my skin prickling with heat. His first notes were tentative.

"Come with me," he sang, faltering on the high notes. *I can't,* Isolde's reply sang in my head.

"Why not?" Karl sang, and I fumbled for the right notes. I didn't know if it was the music or being close to Karl or turning sixteen, but whatever it was, I didn't want to cry. I couldn't let myself cry. Not now, not after all I'd been through, not for a boy. A tear skidded down my cheek.

He reached into his pocket and held out a handkerchief. I stared at it. A perfect square of white cotton, folded into fours. And embroidered in the corner in red stitching, his initials: KJ.

"Keep it," he said.

I shook my head. "It has your initials on it."

He looked at me, puzzled.

"If anyone saw me with it, they'd think I'd stolen it."

His face reddened. He balled up the handkerchief and shoved it into his pocket.

Rosa hovered in the hallway, a rag in her hand. Karl took a seat at the back of the room and pretended to read. I filled the space between us with music. I played Schumann's *Fantasie,* my heart hammering against my chest.

"Why that piece?" Karl asked when Rosa had disappeared up the stairs.

I tried not to blush. "Robert Schumann wrote it for Clara Wieck." I returned the pages to the music cupboard and tidied the shelves so I wouldn't have to look at him.

"They weren't allowed to see each other." *Clara's father didn't want his famous daughter marrying a struggling composer. He took her on tour to keep them apart.* I'd read it so often, I knew the story by heart, every stage of their courtship, the date Schumann proposed, how many days they were kept apart. I never tired of telling it. I closed the cupboard with clammy hands and returned to my seat. "Robert sent her the first movement of the *Fantasie* opus during their separation." *He wrote it for her, had it hand-delivered behind her father's back, and when she played it, Clara knew her fate was sealed.*

I looked down at the piano. Neither of us spoke for a while. Karl stood up and walked to the door. "Wait here."

I sat on my hands. *If he doesn't come back by the time I reach one hundred . . .* I started counting.

He returned with a cup of tea and a custard cake glazed with honey.

"It's left over from yesterday, but it's still good." He held out the plate and saw that I resisted. "I'll set it down here." He placed the plate and the cup on the side table and dragged his chair alongside it. "If anyone comes in, they'll think it's mine."

We both listened for footsteps. The house was quiet, the corridor empty. I lunged at the cake. I tried to eat delicately, to take small bites and chew with my mouth closed, but after the first lick of custard, I gave in. I tore a slab from the cake and shoveled it into my mouth. I turned to Karl, custard dribbling down my chin.

"That's my second piece of cake today." I smiled. It

felt good to smile, but it also felt wrong. Karl looked confused.

"It's my birthday," I said, regretting the words as soon as I'd said them.

"Happy birthday. How old—?"

The grandfather clock in the hall struck midday and Karl stood to leave.

"My singing teacher will be here soon." He gathered up the plates and walked to the door. "Sorry about the handkerchief. It was stupid of me." He looked down at his feet. "Me even being here. It was selfish. I'm sorry."

I spent the afternoon playing Bruckner and Wagner for the commandant and his guests. My fingers found the notes even when my mind was elsewhere. I was in the Puszta forest, picnicking with Karl, and beside him at the opera, and in the park, feeding the ducks. He kept me company all afternoon and on the long walk back to the barrack, but he disappeared at the barbed-wire fence.

I opened the barrack door. It was dark. I was tired. I climbed onto the bunk. Next to me three women huddled together.

"Hanerot halalu anachnu madlikin."

I recognized the whispered prayer. The woman next to me was reciting a Hanukkah prayer in Hebrew, a blessing my mother made every year over the Hanukkah candles. We'd light the candles and eat doughnuts sprinkled with sugar, in celebration of the miracle of the burning oil. I reached under my bunk.

"Here," I whispered, handing the woman the stub of the candle Erika pretended to light for my birthday.

"Baruch Atah Adonai Eloheinu . . ." She pulled a matchbox from beneath her bunk, struck the one remaining match, and lit the wick. It sparked and fizzed, but failed to light.

"Hashem, God of our fathers." The woman held the blackened wick above her head and returned to her prayers. "We light this light for the miracles and wonders you bestowed upon our forefathers." The women next to her repeated the prayer, their fingers outstretched toward the burned-out wick. I looked at their faces alight with hope and wished I could find the comfort they sought.

"When the Maccabees went to the temple to light the Menorah, they found only enough oil for one day."

"One day," the women echoed, their faces shiny with hope.

"One day," the woman with the wick whispered into the dark. "But the oil lasted eight."

Chapter 13

"The commandant won't be needing you to play piano this morning. He has important business to attend to and doesn't want to be distracted." Rosa stopped me in the hallway. "I'm sure you'll find something to do. The commandant's son is already in the music room."

Karl was bent over a battered cardboard box, his hands buried in tinsel. A small tree stood unadorned in the corner of the room.

I opened the music cupboard and pulled out a rag. Another day of dusting. I bent over the piano and ran the rag over the keys. The commandant had come to the music room only once in the last two weeks. I hoped his absence had something to do with the recent fireworks over Birkenau. The block leader said the Russians were coming to save us. The barrack windows had rattled and the sky had glowed orange, but the Russians never came.

"Is the commandant entertaining tonight?" I looked down at the thumb I'd scraped on the rough wood of my bunk and hoped I wouldn't have to play piano. I could still see the dark tip of a splinter buried under my skin.

"No. He's on his way out. It'll just be the two of us." He hunched over the box. It was just the two of us now, and Karl still wouldn't look at me.

"Why won't you look at me? Is it this?" I asked, peeling my scarf from my head.

"No." Karl looked wounded. "Of course not."

I tugged the scarf back over my head.

"It's just . . ." Karl tunneled deeper into the tinsel. "When I look at you, I see what we've done."

"I don't hate you," I said.

"I know." He stared at the box. "You hate Birkenau. I hate it, too. I thought I could hide here, that if I didn't leave the house and go over there"—he looked in the direction of the camp—"I could pretend it didn't exist." He looked down at his feet. "And then you arrived." He stood up and brushed the tinsel from his trousers. A strand of silver ribbon clung to his shirt. He pulled his sketch pad from the side table, opened it to the last page, and walked toward me. I stopped dusting. When he reached the piano, he pulled the stool out and placed the sketch pad on it.

"I did this a while ago." Patches of red spread over

his cheeks. I looked down at the open book. On the last page was a drawing, done in charcoal, of a girl with large pale eyes. She was half hidden in shadow, so you couldn't see her hair or her clothes, but you could tell she was beautiful. Her skin was infused with light, her lips parted in a secret smile.

"She's beautiful," I whispered, turning to Karl.

He looked down at the drawing. "Of course she's beautiful." He brought his face close to mine. "She's you."

"Sorry to interrupt." Rosa stepped from the shadow of the doorway. Karl reached for the sketchbook and flipped it shut. "I just wanted to see if Master Jager wanted a fresh pot of tea?" She didn't look sorry. And when she said it, she wasn't looking at Karl; she was staring at me.

"No, thank you." Karl put the sketch pad into a cupboard and reached for the box of ornaments. Rosa frowned at me and walked back to the kitchen. I ran my rag over the piano. Karl pulled a silver angel from the cardboard box and brushed his fingers along its glinting wings. Neither of us spoke, but it didn't matter. I wasn't invisible. I'd never been invisible. Karl had been watching me from the start, enough to memorize the slant of my nose, the slope of my eyes, the way the light fell on my skin.

"Karl!" the commandant's footsteps echoed down the hall. I ran to my corner. "Ah, you're here!" he said, stepping into the music room. "Decorating the tree? Good. You'll be busy. I'm going out." Karl didn't answer. "Don't sulk," the commandant said. "I haven't forgotten it's Christmas. You'll get your present."

"So you won't be back till late?" Karl asked.

"No. I have a meeting and then a function in town. I've given Klaus and the others the night off, too. It's Christmas Eve, after all." His eyes landed on me. "You!" he waved a finger in my direction. "Find something useful to do."

I ran to the music cupboard.

When I could no longer hear the commandant's heavy footfall, I turned to Karl. He sat crossed-legged on the floor, surrounded by silver-foil snowflakes and hand-painted baubles. He looked wretched. I opened my mouth to speak, but he shook his head and dug deeper into the box. I tried not to look hurt.

"He might not have left yet." He craned his neck to look through the window. "It's—" Outside, a car rumbled to life, gravel spitting from its wheels.

"I know," I interrupted. "It's dangerous." I knew what his father was capable of; I didn't need reminding.

"You don't know the half of it." He planted the angel at the top of the tree. "Here, take these to the kitchen." He pulled three plates from the side table, stacked them one on top of another, and handed them to me. On the plates was a smear of a cream, half a square of marzipan, and three glazed cherries. He lifted the teapot from the table and poured the leftover tea into a cup. "Wash this, too," he said balancing the cup on the plates. I winced.

He looked down at the plates.

"The food," he whispered. "Eat it in the kitchen."

I put the plates on the piano stool and showed him my hand. "It's my thumb. It's sore."

"Have you had it seen to?" He touched the swollen skin. "It looks infected." His forehead creased. "Father is having guests over tomorrow. He'll expect you to play."

He was right, of course. I had to get the splinter out. The commandant was out for the rest of the day. If I slipped away now and went to the infirmary, no one would know.

"I'll go to the infirmary," I said.

"No." Karl shook his head. "Not the infirmary. You have to get it seen to, but not there. Maybe I'll try—"

"It's too deep," I said. "And I'll need something for the infection."

"Then find someone in the camp."

"Who?" I fought to keep my voice low. "Unless your

159

Dr. Huber makes house calls, there *is* no one else."

Karl was silent. I turned for the door.

"The infirmary's not safe, Hanna." Karl blocked the doorway. "It's not like a regular—"

I cut him off.

"My mother's in the infirmary."

We stood there awkwardly. Neither of us spoke. "See the doctor, then leave." Karl stepped away from the door to let me pass.

Outside, the sky was the color of snow, and the ground was glazed with ice. I hurried back to camp with a guard at my back, careful not to trip on the frozen ground. The guard left me standing outside a barrack, and a nurse let me in. The infirmary was cold—a long narrow ward lit by open skylights and crammed with bunks. A rough wooden counter ran between the bunks, its surface littered with buckets of dirty water, excrement, and medicine. Half-naked women lay shivering on the straw mattresses, bones wrapped in skin. I scanned their faces, looking for my mother, but she wasn't among them. Neither was Vera.

I walked toward a door at the far end of the barrack where a line of women gathered, waiting to be seen. A nurse shaved my head. She didn't take my temperature or ask me what hurt. I slipped my silk scarf back over my head.

"The doctor will see you now." The girl at the front of the line limped through the door. Her leg was wrapped in a bloodied rag. I took a step forward. The woman in front of me turned and looked at me, at my silk scarf and my warm winter coat. She had a growth on her neck the size of a tennis ball.

"What are you in for?" She spoke Hungarian.

"My thumb," I answered. "I have a splinter."

"A splinter?" She laughed. "You're here about a splinter! I can barely swallow." She pointed to the lump on her neck.

"I play piano for the commandant," I mumbled. "I have to look after my fingers."

"The commandant?" She grabbed me by the collar and pulled me to her. Her breath smelled rotten. "She plays piano for the commandant," she called out to the women next to her. "I hope they cut both her hands off." She pushed me to the floor. Someone spat at my head. Another woman shoved me; hands reached for my scarf. I scrambled to the back of the line, where they couldn't see me. A girl whose head was too big for her body asked how I'd come by my coat. I told her I stole it.

There was yelling from the other side of the door. I clasped my hands over my ears to dull the sound and tried not to think about losing a finger. Robert

Schumann had his piano career cut short after he'd injured his hand. He'd taken up composing. If I couldn't play, my alternative was the quarry.

The line limped along. We moved forward slowly.

"See you on the other side." The girl in front of me smiled nervously. She was ushered into a room. The door closed behind her. I pressed my ear to the wood. I heard mumbling, footsteps, a muffled cry, then nothing. The minutes wore on.

"Come in." A nurse opened the door and ushered me into a white tiled room. In the center of the room was a hardwood table, and under it, on the floor, four pieces of rope.

"What are you here for?" she asked. I showed her my hand.

"Get undressed and climb onto the table."

I did as I was told. I lay down and waited, the wood cold against my skin. I wiped my nose with the back of my hand. I'd never been to a doctor without my mother. *Where are you, Anyu?* I squeezed my eyes shut. *Papa, I need you.* My father had told me to brave. I forced my eyes open. He'd told me to remember every detail of the camp and tell the world what I'd seen. I looked at the nurse, watched as she wound a length of rope around my right arm and fixed it to the table, then my right leg, and my left. A man entered the room. He was holding a kitchen knife, the type Anyu used for slicing beef. There was a sink in the corner of the room, but he didn't stop to wash his hands. He stepped toward me, holding the knife, its sharpened edge glinting in the fluorescent light. I tried to lift my head to speak, but there was a hand pressing down on my skull and then the doctor leaned over me and the room started spinning.

I woke up in a bed in another white-walled room. I tried to move my thumb, but I couldn't feel anything. My whole hand, from my wrist to the tips of my fingers, was wrapped in gauze. My thumb. I needed to see my thumb. I tore at the bloodstained bandage, struggling to unravel the wet cotton with one hand. I looked around frantically for someone to help.

"Please," I said to the girl lying next to me. I held out my hand.

"Bastards!" she said, struggling to pull the sheet from her bed. "Butchers!" she yelled, tossing the soiled sheet to the floor. She looked down at her legs. "I walked in here with a sore foot. Now look at me! "

I looked down at her legs, one pale and thin, the other a bandaged stump, cut off at the knee.

I leaped out of bed and ran from the infirmary, tearing at my bandage. By the time I reached our barrack, it was dark. I collapsed on the ground outside the hut, squeezed my eyes shut, and peeled off the last layer of gauze. I lowered my hand to my skirt, looked up at the sky, and let my fifth finger graze the fabric. I still had G. I watched the shivering stars and pressed down with my fourth finger, F, then continued the scale, E, D and finally, C. Five notes. Five fingers. I looked down at my thumb. A small piece of flesh had been gouged from the tip. I ran my finger along the incision, careful not to unpick the neat black seam the doctor had stitched into my skin. My beautiful, lacerated thumb. It was pink and tender, but it would heal.

Chapter 14

I pushed the door open and walked over to where the block leader stood.

"I'm sorry. I don't have any food for you tonight."

The block leader glared at me.

"I had to go to the infirmary," I hurried to explain, showing her my hand. The block leader looked down at my swollen thumb, grabbed it between her leathery fingers, and squeezed.

"What are you doing?" I cried, sinking to my knees. The block leader loosened her grip, but she didn't let go.

"I might ask the same of you."

I looked at her blankly.

"A little birdie tells me you've made friends at the villa. One friend in particular. A boy." She dug her fingernails into my skin. "How could you? After all I've done for you." Spit gathered at the corners of her mouth. "Haven't I looked after you? When you got that job at the villa, the women here wanted to tear you to shreds." She turned to the women who had gathered behind her. "I held them back. Made sure you were safe. And this is how you repay me?" She crouched down on one knee and brought her face close to mine. "I confided in you. I told you about my husband and my—" She let go of my hand and stood up. "And then you go and screw one of them."

I stared up at her in horror.

"I haven't—" I began, but Erika pushed past me. Her bony arms hung by her sides. Her feet were bare.

"Leave her alone," she said, stepping between me and the block leader.

The block leader laughed. "What are you going to do? Make me?" She elbowed Erika aside to stand in front of me. "Get out. There's no room for traitors or whores in this barrack."

I clambered to my feet. Erika put her hand on the block leader's shoulder. Her eyes shone in the dim light.

"I'm not going to fight you," she said, walking around to face her. "I don't need to. What do you think my sister's boyfriend will do to you when he finds out you've thrown her out?" She brought her face close to the block leader's. "He'll come after you. Repeat a word of what you've just said or lay a finger on my sister, and he *will* find out. I've made sure of it."

Erika took me by the hand and led me back to our bunk. She didn't let go of my hand, not till a long time later, when her hands had finally stopped shaking.

I lined up for roll call next to Erika. We stood under the frozen clouds, our heads glistening, our breath making ghostly shapes in the dark. The girl next to us collapsed. She was so light, she hardly made a dent in the snow. The guards dragged her away.

"I don't remember what it feels like to be warm." We walked back to the barrack. Erika's feet were purple with cold, her fingers frozen. I drew my coat around her.

"It feels like a standing ovation," I said, "or breakfast in bed on your birthday."

"Or a kiss?" Erika stopped in front of our bunk.

"I wouldn't know," I said, forcing myself to meet her gaze.

"I knew it wasn't true," Erika said, holding her thin arms out.

The block leader called lights out, and the room went black. I hugged my sister and burrowed my head into her bony neck.

"That was low, even for her, accusing you of sleeping with the commandant's son. She had to know how that would make the other women feel."

I shivered.

"It's okay. They won't touch you, not after what I said." Erika eased me from her neck and held my face in her hands. "I hope you didn't mind . . . me calling him your boyfriend. . . . It was the only way. . . ."

"I like him," I said.

Erika pulled her hands from my face. I could hear her breathing quicken in the dark.

"Who?"

"Karl." I couldn't lie to Erika. Not anymore.

We were both quiet.

"I know he's helped you, Hanna," she said eventually. "I know he's been kind, but that's not love. That's gratitude. You don't owe him anything." She sounded angry.

"I know."

"His father is—"

"I know," I said, burying my head in my hands. "I know."

Erika didn't say anything for a long time. I didn't care what the other women thought of me. I didn't care whether they talked to me or talked about me behind my back. I accepted their contempt. Compared to them, I had it easy. But not Erika. I couldn't have Erika think badly of me.

"Please," I whispered, but she cut me off.

"Look, I know it's been hard for you, and maybe Karl can't stand living at the villa, either. You both needed an escape, but that doesn't make it—"

"No. You're wrong," I said, feeling bruised. "It's not about escape. It's him. . . . He's sensitive and he's talented and he understands music. . . ." I touched my hand to my cheek. "I'm blushing just talking about him. I don't blush in the showers or the latrine, but when I'm near him, I don't know." I turned away. "My skin feels hotter, my palms get clammy, and I don't even know if he feels the same way." I buried my head in the mattress.

Erika didn't reach out to me. She didn't say anything. She flung my coat from her body and turned the other way.

"Merry Christmas, Hans." Lagerführerin Holzman handed the commandant a box wrapped in red and gold crepe paper.

"How long has it been?" Captain Jager asked.

"Since my last visit? Five months, maybe six." The *Lagerführerin* smiled. "You were looking for a pianist. I brought you some girls."

169

"Yes, of course, the audition." The commandant put down the gift and poured himself a drink. "There were six girls. Karl picked her." The commandant glanced at me.

Lagerführerin Holzman shrugged off her fur coat, sat down, and crossed her silk-stockinged legs. She was wearing a navy-blue suit and pearls. The war had been good to her.

"It's nice to hear music in your house again, Hans." I was playing Schumann's *Widmung,* a love letter to Clara that was full of sweetness and despair. My thumb was tender, but I'd get through the day. The commandant drained his glass and picked up his baton.

"We used to do this every Christmas, didn't we — you and Max, me and Hilde?" He whispered the words, his eyes strangely slack. "She loved to play." He spoke in a faraway voice, as if the words came from a place deep inside, a place rarely visited.

Karl stood in the doorway, staring at his father. The commandant refilled his glass and loosened his tie.

"Ignore him. He's always lurking around the house, aren't you, son? Lurking around and looking miserable." He drained his drink again, and Karl sat down.

"It's the war." The commandant's face hardened. "My son thinks we're losing it. I tell him not to listen to rumors, but still he mopes." He refilled his glass and swilled it around. "Where's that daughter of yours?"

"Sorry, Captain Jager. I was just outside, admiring your garden." A girl, not much older than me, appeared at the door. She was a carbon copy of her mother, tall and lean, with the alabaster skin of a film star. She had painted lips and painted nails, and long, loose curls framing her face.

I touched my head scarf.

"Karl, say hello to Frau Holzman's daughter." The commandant nudged his son.

"Hello," Karl said.

"Hello." The girl smiled. "I'm Marthe." She unbuttoned her coat and slipped her arms from the sleeves. "I've heard so much about you." She extended her hand.

I leaped into Wagner to drown out the girl's voice. I missed Karl's reply—Wagner's Sonata in B-flat was best played fortissimo—but something shifted in his face, and he shrank back in his chair. When the music dipped and I could hear them again, the commandant was talking about his son's paintings.

"Karl, why don't you take Marthe up to your room and show her your watercolors?"

Karl looked at Marthe, and I belted the keys.

The commandant lifted his baton and struck the piano.

"I can't hear myself think." He struck the lid, then the keys. "Your music is to melt into the background. Continue to play as if this were a concert hall and it'll be your last performance." He turned to his guests. "Now, where were we? Ah, yes, Karl, you were going to take Marthe to your room."

I took a deep breath and returned to the sonata. Piri had always said, if you're nervous, find one person in the audience and play for them. I didn't know who Piri played for when she performed for the SS, but I chose Karl.

"I'd rather listen to music." Karl's eyes flickered toward me. Marthe's mouth sagged. I bit my lip so I wouldn't smile and played Beethoven's *Moonlight Sonata*, hoping Karl would understand. I played it softly, daring him to listen.

"Karl sings, you know." The commandant's voice cut through the closing bars. He turned to his son. "Sing for our guests."

He had me play "Ave Maria." I played Schubert's notes, and Karl sang the words. A pitch-perfect baritone, just as I'd remembered. But there was something else in his singing, something new, a shimmering in the top register, a dark power in the lower notes. An urgency I hadn't noticed before.

I didn't look up from the keyboard until the last refrain. The commandant was sitting in the front row, the *Lagerführerin* behind him. He was leaning forward in his seat, muttering into the carpet, his fingers at his temple, his face glazed with sweat. I'd kept my head down. I'd been careful. He couldn't have guessed I was playing the song for Karl. The commandant rose from his chair.

"I have a headache," he said, lurching toward the piano. "No more music." He pointed his baton at me, then laid it down on the lid. "Go home."

The commandant stumbled from the room.

Karl turned to Lagerführerin Holzman. "I'm sorry, but I have to arrange for the girl's escort."

I slipped from the piano, bowed to the *Lagerführerin,* and followed Karl from the room. We walked down the hallway, through the kitchen, and out the back door into the still, muddied light, the two of us standing there under the same square of sky.

"How did you know?" Karl stopped under the snowy branches of the weeping willow.

"Know what?" The guard at the front gate had his back to us and his scarf wrapped around his ears, but I whispered anyway.

"The *Moonlight Sonata*—it's my favorite." His cheeks

flushed, and then he looked at me—not past me, or through me, but at me. It was like stepping into the spotlight from a darkened stage.

"I'm sorry I can't walk you home." He shifted from one foot to the other, and then the guard turned around and Karl's smile fell away.

I walked back to camp, pulling Karl's words apart and putting them back together, trying to piece together the puzzle of his affection. After a time, I couldn't remember what he'd said, only what I wanted him to say—that I was more to him than a Jew in need of saving.

It was dark by the time I reached Birkenau. The cold gnawed at my fingers and clung to my skin. I saw Michael Wollner in a column of boys heading back to camp. He saw me and smiled, but I couldn't smile back. I turned away, but everywhere I looked there were more Michael Wollners—stick-thin boys in blue-and-white rags with heads like peeled onions and limbs like twigs. Boys who might never fall in love or be kissed. I'd left the villa thinking about Karl, imagining what it might feel like to touch and be touched by him. I watched the dark, skeletal boys disappear into the steel-gray dusk, and I felt like a traitor.

Chapter 15

"They're losing the war," I told Erika as I huddled against her for warmth. The wind whistled through the cracks in the barrack walls, and the cold crept into our beds. An airplane roared overhead. "It's the Russians. They're coming. Everyone's talking about it." Erika didn't raise her head from the mattress. "The commandant's miserable," I persisted. "He must know it's over."

The commandant had asked me to play only twice in the last week, and when he did, he had me play military marches with rousing crescendos in strict 4/4 time. Karl stayed away from the music room. He hated the music his father had me play. I hated it, too, mostly for the transformation it wrought on the commandant. He'd enter the room sullen and exhausted and leave an hour later, galvanized for battle. Karl and I spoke less; the house was too quiet. The officers who assisted the commandant moved soundlessly through the rooms, and the soldiers who guarded the villa patrolled the grounds like bloodhounds. People skulked around with dour expressions. No one made small talk.

"So the Russians are coming. When? Tomorrow? Next week?" Erika shrugged. "I can't wait another month." She pulled herself up to rest on an elbow. She looked pale and worn. Her eyes were glassy, and she was hot to the touch. I wanted to stroke her forehead, but I kept my hands by my sides. She was still angry about Karl.

She lay back on the bed, and her eyes drifted shut. When her breathing slowed and I was certain she'd fallen asleep, I lay down next to her and closed my eyes.

I dragged my sister out of bed the next morning, washed her face, and helped her dress. I made her promise she'd march to the quarry and march back again. I promised her green beans and turnips for dinner. I asked her to be brave.

"I'm tired of being brave. I'm tired of being hungry." She clawed at her scalp and stepped into the breakfast line. "We lug rocks from one side of the quarry to the other. Then they march us to the same spot and make us drag the rocks back again."

"So, drag them back. You've lasted this long," I whispered.

"Drag them back?" Erika grabbed my arm. The women around us turned and stared. "What would you know about lugging rocks? You sit at the piano all day in front of a goddamn fire."

"Not you, too," I said, but in truth I'd been waiting for this moment, expecting it. "I didn't ask to audition. You told me to. You told me to do it to feed Anyu." I dragged Erika away from the food line. "I didn't know things would turn out like this."

Erika peeled my fingers from her arm and stepped back into line. I looked at my sister. She was the only other person who'd heard the same bedtime stories as me, camped in the same forests, eaten the same meals. I couldn't do this without her. What I'd wanted to say to her was that we were meant to survive. That prisoner at the station—the one with the weeping eye—he had told me to say I was sixteen. Then Mengele had pointed us both to the left and we got to share a barrack. I won the commandant's audition even though I wasn't the best pianist. We had extra food. We were *meant* to survive.

The SS closed the quarry the next day. When I told Karl our barrack was to be deployed to a nearby factory, his face crumpled. He fled from the music room and returned a few hours later looking relieved and exhausted. He'd persuaded his father that he needed piano accompaniment to practice for an upcoming performance.

"You're not going with them. I've arranged everything."

"But I have to go. I want to go." I fought to keep my voice low.

Karl look confused.

"It's already done. Father's contacting the camp authorities as we speak."

I should have been flattered. Karl had intervened on my behalf. He'd lied to his father to keep me close. He didn't want me gone, even for a day. And part of me *was* flattered; part of me was thrilled. But I was also angry. My sister needed my help. I wanted to be with Karl, but I needed to be with Erika, especially now, when things were so fragile between us.

"Tell him your plans changed. Tell him I don't want to accompany you. He'll send me back to camp and then I can be with Erika."

"No." Karl shook his head. "He won't send you back. He'll . . ." His eyes jerked up to the window. His father was outside, calling to his driver. Karl looked at me.

"You don't know my father. You don't know what he'll do."

"So tell me."

Karl exhaled. "I had a nanny," he began slowly. "Father hired her to care for me after my mother died. He was never around." He walked to the window and stared out at the bare branches of the plum tree. "Liesl raised me. She took me to the park and to concerts. She taught me to read and draw and sing. I loved her. He knew that." His breath fogged up the pane. "He joined the SS when I was six, and a few weeks later, he sent me to stay with my grandparents. When I got back, she was gone. Her room was empty." He turned to face me, the words spilling out of him. "When I asked my father where she was, he said that she'd lied to us. That she was a Jew, as if that explained everything." His face flushed with anger. "I've never forgiven him."

"I'm sorry," I said.

"I don't want your pity." His anger drained away. "I just need you to understand what kind of man he is. He sent Liesl away. Think what he'd do to you if . . ." He shook his head. "She was the closest thing I had to a mother." He closed his eyes, and when he opened them again, he looked lost.

"What happened to your mother?"

"She died a long time ago." He took a seat at the back of the room and pulled a silver chain from his pocket. Dangling at the end of the chain was an antique silver locket. "I have a photo of her." He held up the locket. "I found it buried under some papers in my father's desk." He pressed a catch on the side of the heart-shaped locket, and it sprang open. "My father's photo was on this side." He pointed to the left side of the locket. It was empty. On the right was a black-and-white photo of a beautiful woman with pale eyes and glossy hair. "That was my mother, Hilde. It's the only photo I have of her." He shut the clasp and slipped the necklace into his pocket.

His only photo? There were no picture frames in the hallway, and no personal photos in the music room. I'd just assumed the commandant and Karl stockpiled their memories upstairs.

"The commandant won't let me go," I told Erika as we stepped from the barrack. It was the morning of our hike to the factory, and our toes were already numb. She seemed relieved.

I made her take my coat. I did up the buttons, pulled the collar close around her neck. She was so small and so frail. She used to tower over me, fill a room, turn heads. "About Karl," I began, but she shook her head. I followed her to the main gate and watched her drag her feet through the snow until she grew smaller and smaller and the fog swallowed her up. I turned toward Osweicim. In an hour, I'd be in front of a roaring fire and she'd still be out here, in the cold, on her own.

The commandant was already in his study when I arrived at the villa. His door was open, and SS officers were pulling documents from his filing cabinets, running outside with them and setting them alight. Gunfire erupted in the distance. The Russians had to be close. I slipped into the music room, grabbed a rag, and started dusting. The wind howled through the open front door, and snowflakes settled on the polished floors. *Erika was out there.*

When Karl walked into the music room, I couldn't look at him. I rehearsed a Chopin sonata in my head to ease the silence, from the stormy opening to the end of the third movement—the funeral march.

"I'll go if you like." Karl waited for a moment. I walked to the cupboard, threw in the rag, and shut the door. I didn't answer him. I let him walk out the door. It was easier that way. Better for everyone.

I spent the rest of the day counting the minutes until I could return to the barrack. The walk home was torturous. I followed the guard into the shower block, changed into my old dress, ran the last steps to our barrack, and flung the door open. The room was empty. I checked the camp square and the latrines. I checked the huts to our left and the barracks on our right. Erika wasn't in any of them. Neither was the block leader, the green triangles, nor any of the other women with whom we slept. I returned to our barrack and waited. No one called me for roll call, and no one brought dinner. I crawled onto the floor and sat by the door, grinding my teeth. I hummed Ravel's *Gaspard de la Nuit*, but I couldn't get inside the music. The sky turned black and still no one came. I grabbed a blanket, kicked the door open, and sat on the steps in the moonless cold, looking out. There were no spirals of smoke floating up from the chimneys. No truck tires spitting gravel. No guards with guns. Just the startling cold. I left the door open and waited for Erika, but she never came.

No one did.

Chapter 16

I don't know who found me shivering in the doorway, or what time of day it was when I was dragged from the barrack to another hut, three doors down. The new block leader introduced herself and assigned me a bunk. I stood at the window, wrapped in a blanket, and stared out at the charcoal sky.

"They're not coming back."

I turned from the window to see who had spoken. A girl with jutting-out bones and a pointy nose sat up in her bunk. She was all angles—gangly arms hanging from her narrow shoulders, and a head too large for her pale, thin neck. "We're all that's left." She motioned to the women lying next to her, their eyes empty, their bodies still. My mother wasn't among them. I turned back to the window. The camp square was deserted, the watchtowers empty. The door of the barrack opposite swung on its hinge. No one was inside. An elderly woman in rags walked between the barracks, her body bent against the wind. An SS officer hurried past.

"Where is everyone? Where've they gone?" I asked the girl.

"I don't know. I was in barrack 12. We were told we were hiking to a factory, so I snuck in here."

"My sister went with them," I said. "They were meant to come back last night." My legs were shaking. I reached for a bunk and sat down.

"There are no factories." The block leader stood before us, her thin arms crossed over her drooping chest. "The SS are leaving because they know the Red Army is on its way, and they've taken everyone with them—everyone who's still useful to them, anyway. They didn't clear out the infirmary." She looked around the room. "Or take us. Probably didn't think we'd make it."

"Make it?"

"To the other camps. Word is they're headed north."

"Other camps? How far away?"

She looked at me with something resembling sympathy.

"Three days' walk, maybe four."

I ran to the door and pushed it open. I staggered outside, pulled off my boots, and stood in my flimsy dress, barefoot in the ankle-deep snow. I let the wind whip my cheeks and the cold seep into my bones.

Erika was out there somewhere. She didn't have boots, a scarf, or mittens. Four days . . . I took one step, then another. My feet grew numb, but I walked on till I couldn't feel my fingers or my face or the pain in my chest. I walked past the watchtower to the main gate.

A guard stopped me. "You're the commandant's girl?"

I nodded dumbly.

"You want to head left, then, not right. Has the commandant sent for you?" He looked confused.

"Yes," I said. "Yes, he did."

He looked down at my feet and shook his head. "I can't deliver you like that. Go find some shoes."

The villa was deserted. A lone guard stood at the front gate, his eyes on the road, his hand on his gun. There were no cars in the driveway, no guards in the hall. Rosa wasn't lurking on the stairs, and Ivanka wasn't at the sink. Mr. Zielinski was gone, too. The house was dark. I crept along the silent corridors and stopped at the open door of the commandant's study. The desk was empty and the bookshelves bare. I picked up the wastepaper basket.

"There's nothing in there. I already checked."

I spun around. Karl was standing in the hallway. He grabbed my hand and pulled me to the music room.

"My father's gone to Kraków. They've all left." He reached for the drapes and pulled them apart. "Except for him," he said, pointing to the guard at the gate.

"You knew, didn't you?" I stepped toward him.

"I tried to tell you yesterday."

"You should have. I could've done something for Erika." I stood in front of him. "*You* could've done something. . . ." Karl hung his head. "You're the commandant's son. You can do whatever you want." He didn't answer. "You say you hate the war." My temper flared. "But I don't believe you!" I knew that what I said made no sense, but it felt good to fight back. Good to blame someone other than myself.

"I tried. I'm sorry." His voice was so low, it was almost a whisper.

"No, you're not," I said. "If you were sorry, you'd be out there doing something to get her back." I grabbed his shirt. "It's not too late. You could get a car and a driver. You could find out where they are." I was still holding on to his shirt, the cotton crushed between my fingers, my hands balled against his chest. "She's all I have left." I slumped against him. "You *have* to help. You *have* to save her." The sky sparked white, and the windows rattled. Karl looked at me and shook his head.

"I can't."

"Can't?" I ran from the room. I flung the front door open and stepped onto the porch. It was bitterly cold, but I couldn't go back inside, not with Erika out there. I ran onto the road and tramped through the snow, sinking deeper into the drifts with each step. The villa disappeared and then the street signs, too. I stood in the blinding white, tears dripping from my chin, not knowing whether to head left or right. I didn't see Karl until he was by my side. His hair was speckled with snow, his shirt wet.

"Come inside," he begged, pulling me to him.

I didn't take his hand, but I followed him home. I sat at the piano without opening the lid, facing away from him, too exhausted to speak. I didn't know what to say, so I didn't say anything. I didn't know what to do, so I sat there, mute.

Karl set a cup of tea down on the table beside me and draped a blanket over my legs.

"I can go." His words said one thing; his face another. I nodded. I didn't want to talk. My sister was out there, either walking through a snowstorm or buried under one. I kicked off the blanket and pushed the tea away. Karl's shoulders slumped. He picked up the blanket and walked out of the room.

* * *

"I'm sorry, I know you don't want company," Karl peered in from the hallway. It might have been an hour later. Maybe more. Time had spun away from me. "My father called. He won't be back for two days."

I looked at him blankly.

"You don't have to stay."

I stood to leave.

"Or you could stay. We could look in the kitchen for something to eat." He looked down at the dirty cup hooked to my belt.

"No," I said, though my stomach was rumbling. "I need to get back." I stood and walked to the door. I couldn't stay here by the fire when Erika was out there.

"The Russians are close." Karl followed me. "The SS are dismantling the camp and heading west." I stopped at the door. "I heard my father on the telephone. The prisoners left by train. Maybe your sister's with them." I let go of the doorknob. They went by train. If Erika made it to the train station, she might still be alive.

"Can I show you something?" Karl spoke quickly. "In my room?"

I hesitated. Karl glanced at the door. "It's locked. The guard can't come in."

I followed him up the stairs. In all my time at the villa, I'd never risked going up the stairs. Karl stopped at a door and turned the handle. Stepping over the threshold was like being sucked back to the past. It was like stepping into my own room and my life before the war. There was an open fire, a Persian rug, and a leather armchair, just like Papa's. There was a double bed and a wooden bookcase and an upright piano pushed against a wall.

"An August Förster!" I ran to the piano and threw open the lid. "I had one just like it at home." I sat down and ran my fingers over the keys, lingering at middle C. Karl sat down beside me, his leg resting against mine. I lifted my hands to the keys and played the opening bars of Erika's favorite piece, Ravel's *Gaspard de la Nuit,* and when Karl touched the keys, I shifted my hands up an octave and we played together. It was like dancing a waltz, as intimate as if we'd been running our fingers along each other's bodies, caressing skin instead of ivory.

"Thank you," I said when the song ended.

"For what?"

"For seeing me, when it would have been so easy to only see this. . . ." I looked down at my bony legs and my mud-spattered dress. I pulled up my sleeve and held out my arm. "For calling me by my name, not my number."

"I wish we could have met somewhere else," he

said. "At the symphony, or a dance. If I'd walked up to you and asked you to dance—"

"I would have said yes."

He weaved his fingers through mine.

"You're shivering," he said. "You need a warm drink." I followed him downstairs to the kitchen. He made me a cup of black tea, dropped a cookie onto a plate, and slipped another into my pocket. The grandfather clock in the hall struck two.

Karl's smile faded. "You should go." He pulled off his scarf and draped it over my neck.

I hesitated.

"Go home, Hanna."

"Home?"

Karl nodded. "You'll be free soon. Go back to Debrecen. Find your family."

"Come with me," I said, surprised by my own daring.

"I can't," he said. "I'm the son of the commandant." There was fear in his voice—sadness, too.

"I'll tell them you saved my life. I'll tell them . . ."

Karl shook his head.

"It's not just that. If you go back to Debrecen and find your parents, how will you introduce me? They won't understand, Hanna, and you can't expect them to."

"And if they're not there?" My voice splintered.

"You'll start a new life." He took my hand. "You can't do that if I'm with you, reminding you of your old one. Every time you look at me, you'll be reminded of Birkenau."

"Yes, and the music room at the villa." I leaned in to him. "And our first kiss."

I stood on my toes and brought my face close to Karl's. I'd dreamed of our first kiss. I'd played the scene a thousand different ways, but never like this . . . standing at the front door, saying good-bye. Karl's eyes dropped to my mouth. I could feel his heart pounding through his shirt, but he didn't kiss me. He brushed my cheek with the back of his hand and then he reached up and pulled my scarf from my head. He ran his fingers over my stubbled head, traced the arc of my nose, the dark circles under my eyes. He looked at me, and it didn't matter that my ears stuck out and my scalp glowed white. It didn't matter that my dress was damp and my fingernails were dirty, and for a split second, I almost told him what I was thinking: *I could love you.*

And then he kissed me. Just the faintest brush of his lips against mine. It was like being thrown toward the sun. I waited for it to feel wrong, but it didn't. I thought of the first time I'd sat down at a piano, how wonderful the keys felt under my fingers, how sure

I'd been that nothing else would ever come close to the feeling I had sitting on that stool, making music.

We stood there, holding each other. Neither of us wanting to be the first to let go. I felt more alive, and afraid, than I ever had before.

And then a loud whistling sound tore through the room and the ground shook. Karl grabbed my sleeve and pulled me to the door.

"I don't want you here when the Red Army turns up. Go back to camp, Hanna. You'll be safe there. Please." His breath was jagged. He reached for the door handle.

"Walk around the camp. Go to the bombed buildings hidden behind the trees. Go to the shower block on the other side of the tracks. Talk to people. Find out what we did."

He pulled the door open.

"What your father did." I buried my face in his neck. His skin was streaked with sweat, but I could still smell his musky scent. He stepped away from me and took my hands in his.

"Please," he said, opening the door wide.

"You'll leave, too?" I asked, searching his face. "Before they get here?"

He nodded and closed the door.

Chapter 17

I walked back to camp alone, but Karl was still with me, the warm, woolen scarf he had given me snug around my neck, his tender touch, the warmth of his skin. It seemed that before Karl, I'd known nothing of life.

"Who cleared you to leave camp?" A guard stood at the sentry gate. The sky exploded in oranges and reds.

He pointed his rifle at me.

"The commandant sent for me." The lie came easy. "I'm his pianist." He checked my number against the list on his clipboard and waved me through.

I opened the door to the barrack. A group of women stood huddled around a window. An armored truck rumbled past. The block leader's face was pressed against the glass.

"They're going to put up a fight," she whispered to the women circling the window. "They still have guns." She pulled a wilted cabbage leaf from her pocket and stuffed it into her mouth. I walked outside, snapped an icicle from the barrack's sloping roof, and sucked on it.

"Please, hurry," I whispered to the winter sky. I was talking to the Russians. I was talking to Karl.

I walked inside and lay down and waited for the room to grow dark. I listened to the tanks rumble by and the women whimper in their beds.

I tried to sleep, but my dreams were filled with Erika. Erika being beaten by a guard, Erika bent over a rusted washbasin, Erika marching through the snow—dreams in black and white and gray. Gunfire perforated the silence. I rose from the bunk in the half dark and shuffled to the window. The sky was doused in pink. Flashes of light exploded in the distance, clouds of smoke rising up after them.

I lay there that night and all the next day, waiting for the Russians to come, waiting for someone to return from the march and tell us that our mothers and sisters were still alive. No one came. The women around me died in their beds. Outside, the guards blew up buildings.

At nightfall, I snuck into my old barrack. I found a turnip tucked under the block leader's mattress and a potato in her nightstand, and I ate them raw. I went to my old bunk and ran my hands along the planks, across the empty gray space where Erika used to sleep.

I closed my eyes and tried to recall her face, her dark brown eyes, grown pouchy and deep, the thin skin and sunken cheeks, her shaved head, her brave smile. She'd smiled when I'd told her I was staying behind. Did she know, then, that she wasn't coming back?

At sunrise, I watched my old barrack burn. I was returning from the latrine hut when I saw three guards run from the barrack as it went up in smoke. I should've felt lucky. If I hadn't needed the toilet . . . I stared at the flames. I didn't feel lucky. I felt empty and alone. I hid behind a wall and watched my jail collapse. I'd dreamed so many times of setting the barrack alight, of razing the camp and clawing down the barbed wire and walking out of Birkenau. In my dreams, Erika lit the match and I flung it under a bunk and we escaped the flames—and Birkenau—together. I watched the blue plumes engulf the hut and wondered which barrack would be next.

There was no way to escape. There were still a handful of guards, with grenades and guns, and maybe others in the forest beyond the gates. And even if I made it to the forest, with the fog and swirling snow, I wouldn't know which way was north. I wouldn't have any food.

I drew my blanket around me and crept down the snow-blanketed path to the main square, my thoughts swirling. They're burning the empty barracks. Hiding the evidence. The Russians must be close. In twenty-four hours, the war might be over and my new life begun. I could search for Anyu and Papa. I could leave Birkenau and look for Erika. I'd be free.

I edged closer to the main gate, sheltering behind a barrack so I wouldn't be seen. I peered around the building. There were two guards at the gate and another three standing with their guns cocked. A row of prisoners was lined up against a wall. There was a volley of gunfire. I held my breath and watched them fall: two women with black triangles on their shirts, six with yellow stars, and a child no more than seven with scabs on her knees. I threw up on my boots.

I had to hide. If the guards were looking to kill the rest of us, I had to find a place where no one would look. Flames licked at the roof of the shower block. I ran to the latrine hut and threw the door open. The smell made me retch, but I scrambled over the boggy ground to the back of the hut and climbed into the pit. I pinched my nose between my fingers, curled my knees to my chest, and waited for a soldier with a red star on his cap to pull me out.

I sat listening to the bombs fall, too frightened to venture out. I left the safety of the latrine hut only once, at midday, to spoon a handful of snow into my cup, but returned to spend the next twenty-four hours in the pit with my arms wrapped around my head to shut out the noise. I played concertos in my head to mask the dull thud of walls collapsing and the sound of my own shallow breathing. I played pieces I'd composed for my mother and father, pieces Erika loved, pieces I'd played a thousand times without ever really understanding them — Rimsky-Korsakov's *The Young Prince and Princess,* Tchaikovsky's *Romeo and Juliet.*

Shit clung to my coat and got under my fingernails. The smell hung on my hair and stuck to my skin. I cried myself to sleep. The sun was already high in the sky when I woke the next day. When the spray of machine gunfire thinned and stopped, I climbed from the pit and dragged myself to the door. I heard muffled footsteps and whispered words. I pushed the door open. Two women shuffled past carrying a body between them.

My voice was hoarse. "Where are the guards? Have the Russians come?" They didn't hear me. I stepped outside, dizzy with hunger, and followed them. They tramped through the snow to the far end of a field and swung the limp body between them — once, then twice — before letting go. The body arced into the air, then plummeted, its fall cushioned by another body. The women stepped away, and others took their place, tossing their dead sisters onto the pile.

Prisoners wandered the camp, searching for food. I slipped between the women's barracks, searching for my mother. Most of the huts were empty, their roofs caved in, their walls blackened by fire. The few that still stood were peopled by women and girls too weak to rise from their bunks. They lay on the planks and waited for death.

I walked past a group of women huddled in a burned-out barrack, hacking at a block of gray bread.

"Where did you get that?" I asked, my voice sharper than I'd intended. The women swung around; their eyes traveled down my face to my throat and the scarf looped around my neck. The skinniest of the three closed her fingers around the loaf.

"Tell me where you got that scarf and I'll tell you where I got the bread." She dropped the bread into her lap, pulled a knife from her pocket, and chipped at the frozen crust.

"I haven't eaten in two days." I ignored her question. She sawed through the loaf and divided it among the group.

"So you're hungry." She gnawed on the stump of bread. "My neck is cold. Looks like we're even."

Gunfire erupted in the distance. Up ahead, a truck idled at the main gate, its engine spewing gray smoke onto the snow. A guard clutching a striped shirt to his chest ran past as I lurked in the shadows. He leaped into the waiting truck and pulled the door closed. The gate opened, and the truck sped out. I stepped from behind the hut and watched the truck's taillights recede into the fog. The gate closed.

"Where are you, Anyu?" I whispered into the gloom.

Behind me a knot of women were arguing beside a barbed-wire fence.

"I'm going to find food. You want to join me, then shut up and follow. You want to stay here and starve, that's up to you." A girl stepped away from the group and bent down to survey the fence. She wrapped her hands around a breach in the wire and pulled at the weakened fibers until the hole was large enough to crawl through.

"Don't be foolish, Klara," the women hissed. "Wait till the Russians arrive. You don't know who's out there."

I approached the girl.

"I'll come." I bent down and pulled the wire apart. She crawled through, and I crawled after her, wincing as the barbed wire caught my head scarf. I let it slip from my head and left it shivering in the breeze.

"The guards have deserted." She put a finger to her lips and crouched down. "But it only takes one. . . ." I crouched down and followed her.

"SS quarters," she whispered, pointing to a stand of huts splayed along the fence.

We crept behind the first of the huts, rising onto tiptoe to peer through the window. The guards had left in a hurry. A chessboard sat on a table in the middle of the room, knights poised in battle. Two bowls of soup sat either side of the board, their spoons sticking out. We scrambled through the door, pitched the spoons from their bowls, and slurped down the broth. The guards had fled before draining the tea from their mugs, so we emptied those, too, sucking at the sugar that dribbled down the sides of the cup. Klara found an empty sack on the floor and we swept through the hut, filling the bag with whatever we could find: custard powder, lard, whiskey, potatoes. She pulled an eiderdown from a bed and wrapped it around her body, securing it at the waist with a guard's leather belt. I wrapped a white cotton pillowcase around my head.

We snuck back along the fence, dragging the sack between us, till we saw my silk scarf flapping in the wind. Klara squeezed through the hole first. I pushed the sack through after her and climbed back into camp.

She handed me a bruised potato. I took it and bit into its soft green flesh.

"My mother used to buy potatoes from the market, but they weren't as bitter as this." I forced myself to take another bite. "She bought the baby potatoes, the ones with the white skin. She said they were the secret to her silky mash." I pictured my mother leaning over a bowl of steaming potatoes, peeling each in turn, adding milk and butter, and whisking the mash until it stood in peaks.

I thanked Klara and walked back to the women's camp, past the electrified fences that had separated me from my father for all these months. The gate was open. Papa! I ran through the gate, thinking of all the boys and men locked away from their sisters and mothers and lovers and wives, until today. Papa! My heart quickened.

An old man stood outside a dilapidated hut, his Adam's apple pushing through his thin skin.

"Esther." He reached out a bony hand and grabbed my coat. "Esther, you're alive!" He pulled me into his shuddering body. I didn't pull away. I wrapped my arms around his brittle body and returned to him—if just for a moment—his long-lost daughter or sister or wife.

I slipped from the old man's embrace and continued down the path to look for my father. There were no guards patrolling the grounds, so I swung open doors and peered into storage sheds. I knocked on windows, crawled under bunks, and yelled out Papa's name. I must have called for him a thousand times, until my voice grew faint and I began to lose hope. There were so few men alive and so many dead. They lay collapsed into each other in the shadows of buildings, hidden behind the latrines, and collected in carts. I wanted to look away, but what if Papa was among them and too weak to call out? I scanned their faces for my father's gray eyes, for his dimpled chin and strong, square jaw. I didn't see him.

An airplane screamed low over the camp and the sky filled with flames. I ran back to the barrack, panting. I swung the door open and dived under the bunk, and for the first time in a year, I prayed. I prayed that the angry airplanes that roared over Poland had red stars on them. And that Mama, Papa, Erika, and Karl were somewhere in Poland waiting for the Germans to wave the white flag.

Chapter 18

I lay facedown on the concrete floor under my bunk. My legs were cramping; my fingers were frozen. I was hungry and I needed the toilet. It reminded me of the cramped cattle train. Locked in the slatted box with nothing to eat and no way out, I'd thought that whatever our destination, it had to be better than that stinking carriage. I was wrong.

I fell into a dreamless sleep and woke to the sound of footsteps scurrying across the floor. I pulled myself out from under the bunk and edged toward the window, where a group of women stood pointing excitedly to the main square. I pressed my face to the glass. The place was deserted. A woman in a gray sack dress stood in the middle of the square under a cloudless sky. Others joined her—an old woman with a limp, a little girl wearing a striped shirt hanging down to her ankles, a group of boys looking for their mothers.

The door swung open and a woman in a tattered shirt poked her head into the barrack.

"The last guards have fled their posts," she shrieked, hopping from one birdlike leg to the other. "The watchtower's empty; the sentry post has been abandoned. No more SS . . ." She ran to the next hut.

"No more food," a voice whispered from one of the bunks. I looked up and saw a face poking from a blanket: a girl with gray teeth and eyes as big as saucers. She looked sick; her skin was a dangerous yellow. I reached up and took her hand.

"The Russians will come. They'll bring food."

She looked frightened.

"No more guards!" The girls at the window stared at each other. "No selections!" They shook their heads in disbelief. "No work!" Their eyes widened. "No roll call!" They pulled the door open and stepped onto the snow.

I pulled my hand from the dying girl's grip.

The path leading to the main gate was crawling with inmates. They appeared from behind barracks and under carts, from empty sheds and burned-out buildings, blinking at the sun, dragging themselves to the gate, half naked and wrapped in blankets. They came alone and in pairs, young women grown old and old women dying. They shuffled through the snow, laughing, cursing, praying, crying. Mostly they wandered the square in a daze. All of us were hungry, and everyone was weak.

The girl next to me was the first to notice the four men on horseback.

"The Russians are here!" she yelled, running for the gate. "The Russians have come!"

Four soldiers — gigantic men with long green cloaks and fur hats — leaped from their horses. They had guns slung over their shoulders but they didn't point them at us, and when they stopped at the watchtower and stared into camp, at the burning barracks and the bodies sprawled on the ground, their mouths fell open.

A truck sped through the main gate.

"Friends," the loudspeakers blared in German, Polish, and Yiddish. "You are free. You have been liberated by the Allied Forces."

A strangled cheer rose from the crowd. The girl next to me started crying. The man to my left fell to the ground. Someone hugged me. Two officers had words with a group of Russian inmates, and we fell into line again. This time it was to wait for cookies, soap, and chocolate. I stood in front of an officer with red hair and pink skin and held out my hand. He must've thought me a creature from another planet, because he stared at me for the longest time. I knew what he saw, though I hadn't looked into a mirror for days: a sparrow wrapped in a blanket, a pillowcase on her head; a face caked in dirt; bare legs, dirty fingernails.

"What's your name?" he asked, first in Russian, then German.

"Hanna," I answered, "but they don't use names here." I pulled my sleeve back and showed him my tattoo. He pulled a chocolate bar from a box and handed it to me.

"How old are you?" The question seemed to make him sad.

"Sixteen," I said, sucking at the square of cocoa.

More officers poured into the camp. They leaped from tanks, armored cars, and jeeps, lugging medical supplies, water, and food after them. They set up tents and tables in front of the watchtower, and a desk with papers and pens. They built a fire in the main square and set a pot to boil over it. They threw a pig into the pot with some potatoes and cabbage. A hungry mob swarmed around the pot.

"Give your stomach time to adjust." The block leader pulled me from the line. "Start on bread and crackers. Stick to bland foods." Out of habit, I followed orders, but it was hard reining in my hunger when those around me gorged themselves on meat and cheese. Hard, too, to watch them hours later, clutch their stomachs and soil themselves before they reached the latrines. I'd imagined this moment of freedom so many times, but never like this, never without Erika. I should've been glad, but I couldn't celebrate. Not till I'd found out what had happened to my family. Not until I knew what had happened to Karl.

The Red Army captured their first SS officer that day. They tore off his blue and white disguise, tied his arms behind his back, and threw him against a wall. A group of prisoners gathered around, hissing and cursing and spitting at his feet.

"Let us at him," they begged. But the guards shook their heads and pushed the men back. The prisoners circled and shouted abuse. They scooped rocks from the ground and hurled them at the man's head.

The guards marched him to a barrack. I snuck after them. The moon was hidden behind a cloud, so I couldn't see the officer's face until he was under the floodlights. He looked tired and pale. His hair stuck out at odd angles, and he had a bruise on his cheek. The guards pushed him into the barrack and locked the door. Two Russian soldiers guarded the hut.

"Is he the only one in there?" I approached the soldiers. They looked at me strangely.

"Are there others?" I reached into my pocket and felt for my black C-sharp. My hands were shaking. I closed my fingers around the wood.

"Don't worry about the prisoners. Concentrate on going home."

I didn't want to go home. In the camp there was at least the possibility I might see my parents and Erika, that they might still be alive. If I went home, I'd find out. My father would be in our apartment on the couch, reading the newspaper, and my mother would be in the kitchen, frying fish. Or not. I wasn't ready to stop hoping. I wasn't ready to go back.

I wandered back to the women's camp. Two Polish men walked past dragging huge legs of meat. I followed them to the main square and warmed my hands by the fire that burned in the yard. The men fed the fire with wooden planks, and when they dragged a pot onto the flames, filled it with water, and threw in the meat, I stepped into line and waited to be fed. A woman pushed past me carrying a baby. She stepped to the front of the line and held out her child.

"May I have some?" she asked the man doling out the soup. She pulled the cloth from her child's face. "It's for my son; he's hungry."

The man looked down at the infant, at his blank eyes and black face and slack mouth.

"I'm sorry, but the child's—"

"Thirsty, I know." The woman pressed the shrouded body against the man's chest. "Please, just a little soup. Then he'll stop crying."

The man shook his head, but the woman kept begging.

"If I could feed him, I would, but my milk's dried up." The woman started to pull at her top, but the man stopped her. He held the ladle over the baby's mouth and tipped the broth onto the child's blue lips.

Two Soviet nurses found me collapsed on the snow. They lifted me from the ground and helped me walk to a nearby tent. They opened a can of vegetables and fed me carrots and peas. I let them undress me and run a warm, wet sponge over my body. They shampooed my short hair and toweled it dry. I lifted my arms, and they pulled a nightgown over my head and led me to a cot with clean white sheets and a woolen blanket. I let them have my cup, but I curled up with my black C-sharp.

I slept for a day and a half.

When I woke, I asked if I could stay. Outside the tent's draped walls, peasants stacked the dead and dug graves. Farmers hosed down barracks while their wives handed out clean underwear and toothbrushes.

I wanted to help, too. I needed to do something while I waited for news about my family, and I owed the nurses and the inmates, too. I'd had extra rations at the villa and a roof over my head while they'd survived on spoonfuls of snow.

I fed water to the sick with medicine droppers, and when they were stronger, I held cups to their lips and fed them soup. I crushed up crackers and fed them crumbs. I washed their bodies and rubbed ointment onto their sores. When the woman who'd begged for soup was brought to the tent, I held her baby while she climbed into bed. And when she woke and asked me to help her bury him, I stood beside her and held her hand while the soldiers lowered his body into the ground.

They buried him behind a stand of birch trees, near a bombed-out brick building. Next to the building, a pile of bodies lay frozen in the snow. Inside the ruins, a bank of ovens lined the walls. A woman walked in after me and stared into a furnace, her face smudged with tears. She tore her dress and recited Kaddish, the prayer for the dead. Father had torn his shirt and sung Kaddish when I was six years old, except he'd been standing over Opapa's grave, staring into the hole where his father's casket lay.

I peered into the oven's dark cavity to see what she saw. There was ash and soot, but there was also bone. I felt the ground slip from under me. The strange, hovering smog that I'd noticed the night I got off the train, the smell of charred meat, the smoke that belched from the giant chimneys . . . They'd been burning bodies. And the piles of dead outside — they weren't waiting to be buried. They were waiting to be burned.

I felt like I'd been hit across the head with a piano stool. I pushed past the woman and ran for the door, and when I got outside, I kept running. Past the birch trees and the barracks and the hospital tent until I reached the shower block on the other side of the camp. A boy sat on the steps leading into the changing room. I sat down next to him.

"I've just been over there." I pointed in the direction of the birch trees. "I saw the ovens. I had no idea."

The boy shook his head.

"Please tell me this is a shower block." I tugged on his sleeve. "It looks like a shower block." The boy remained silent. "Please," I whispered.

"They're not showers," he said.

I shifted closer to the boy. I should've left. I should've walked away.

"Not showers?"

"No." He chewed on a fingernail. "They didn't pipe water through the showerheads. They piped gas."

"No, you're wrong," I said, standing to leave.

"I'm not." He spoke slowly, as if to a child. "I worked here." His shoulders slumped. "I locked the doors."

I threw up on the snow. Why had no one told me? Karl knew about the ovens. He must have known about the showers, too. Why didn't he tell me? Erika had said she'd heard rumors, but I hadn't let her tell me. Why didn't she make me listen? Did they think I was too weak? I walked to the nearest hut and flung open the door. I walked from one end of the camp to the other. I climbed through windows and saw bodies crammed into cupboards, and storehouses bursting with shoes. I saw walking sticks and spectacles and canvas bags full of hair.

Hitler meant us to die! We weren't here to dig trenches. We were brought here to die. How had I not seen it in all my months in the camp? The women saying Kaddish, the emptying beds, Lili and Agi.

And me, putting on lipstick and playing piano for the commandant.

I lined my pockets with rocks and stormed from the camp. I wasn't the only one. There were dozens of us

212

looking to even the score. We smashed windows and broke chairs and tore curtains from the walls of the SS officers' quarters. We rampaged through the villages circling the camp. We stole chickens from their coops and threw eggs at farmhouses. We drove nails through truck tires and drove cattle from their paddocks. We pulled washing from lines and pulled down fences. I didn't feel guilty; I felt entitled. I'd passed those farmhouses hundreds of times. Their owners had seen me march through the snow with a gun at my back and they'd done nothing. I wanted them to taste fear. I wanted *them* to be scared.

Chapter 19

We weren't allowed to return to Hungary. The guards told us it wasn't safe. Hungary was still under siege. The Red Army had surrounded Budapest, but the pro–Nazi Arrow Cross gangs still ruled the streets. They roamed the capital, robbing Jews. They beat them in their homes and threw their bodies into the Danube.

The Russians moved us from Birkenau to the nearby Auschwitz camp. We slept in the SS officers' quarters on beds with thick mattresses. It took me a long time to sleep well on those clean, white sheets, to turn on a tap and not be surprised by the gush of clean water. To be called by my name and have people smile at me. I looked down at my arm, at the number in blue ink etched into my skin. I might have survived, but I wasn't free. No matter how hard I tried to erase what happened, I was still marked. Nothing could rub out the past, not even Karl. Especially not Karl. Maybe he was right. Maybe every time I looked at him, I'd be reminded of what his father had done to us. Maybe we couldn't help but drag each other back to this place.

I tried not to think about Karl, but every time I heard someone hum a tune or speak German, I was reminded of him. I hoped working at the camp hospital might help. Anything to keep me busy and stop me from thinking about Karl. And worrying about my parents. And fretting over Erika. On my third day on the ward, I ran into Vera. I was washing the dormitory windows, staring out at the navy sky. I heard her voice before I saw her.

"Has anyone got a sponge they can spare?" she called out, and without even looking, I knew it was her. I jumped down from my ladder and grabbed her by the arm.

"Vera! You're alive!" I wrapped my arms around her.

"Hanna!"

We stood there looking at each other until we both believed it was true: we'd survived. I took her hand and led her outside.

"Did you know?" I asked her, my smile fading.

"Know what?"

"That Mengele sent babies and pregnant women straight from the train to the gas chambers?"

Vera nodded. "Old people, too. My grandmother was one of them. My mother and I were sent to the right and my grandmother to the left." She took a deep breath. "Two weeks later, they took my mother."

"At a selection?"

Vera nodded. "All those men and women picked off, one by one." She shook her head.

"They weren't all sent to the showers?" *Not my mother, not Anyu.*

"No, not all of them." She spoke quietly. "But the SS could only squeeze so many bodies into the barracks and we kept coming, week after week. They had to make space for the new inmates, the ones who could work."

"I was thinking about going home to see who . . ." Bile rose in my throat. "I won't see my mother. That's what you're trying to say, aren't you? That she's dead."

"Your mother . . ." Vera's hand flew to her throat. "I'm so sorry, I forgot." Vera shook her head. "My mother was weak. I think it was typhus. She was dizzy, and when they asked her to hop up and down . . ." Vera covered her face with her hands. "She could barely walk. If she'd been a little stronger, maybe they would have sent her to the infirmary. Maybe your mother . . ." Vera looked up at me. "I don't know, Hanna."

I buried my face in my hands.

"What am I supposed to do?"

"Go home." Vera pulled a handkerchief from her

216

pocket and wiped my nose. "Go back to Debrecen. If your family's alive, they'll be waiting for you."

I shook my head.

"Miracles happen." She blotted my tears. "The day Mengele pointed you to the right, that was a miracle. Winning the audition, watching the Red Army walk through those gates . . . Maybe there's a miracle waiting for you in Debrecen. You need to go home and find out."

"What about Karl?"

"Karl's in a prisoner-of-war camp, being interrogated."

"What?" I stumbled backward. "He was captured? But I was with him. We said good-bye. I came back to camp. The SS were still here." I stared at Vera "He had time to get away." I counted the days in my head. "He had a week."

"The commandant got away." Vera pressed her handkerchief into my palm. "If the Red Army stormed the villa and found Karl there, it was because he wanted to be found."

I left Auschwitz the day the German troops surrendered Budapest. It was a sunny day in February; the snow had finally begun to thaw, and the sky was blue with possibility. I left with a toothbrush, a spare pair of underwear, and the promise of a new beginning. I had a coat, a pair of secondhand boots, Karl's scarf, and a train ticket to Debrecen. I kissed Vera good-bye and promised to keep in touch.

I stopped at the gates of Birkenau on the way to the station, looking through the gaps in the barbed-wire fence at a place I didn't recognize. There were no bodies lying in the snow, no scarves of smoke spiraling from the chimneys. Grass sprouted in the cracks between bricks. Last time I'd stood at the fence, the sky had screamed with fighter planes. Now bees buzzed overhead. Last time, my head had been covered with bristles. Now my hair skimmed my ears. I was wearing a dress without a yellow star on it, and in my bag I had three plums, a loaf of rye bread, and a thermos of water.

The barracks had been flattened, but I didn't need the windowless walls and corrugated iron roofs to navigate my way through the camp. I could still see the imprint of the shower block where I'd scrubbed myself clean and the burned-out remains of the barrack I'd shared with Erika. I knew the exact spot where the orchestra had plucked their strings, and in which corner of the yard the SS had erected their gallows. I ran to the shower block where they'd stripped us of our clothes and stopped at the step leading into the showers. I bent down, reached under the wooden slats, and pulled out Erika's film canister. The tin was rusted, but its lid was fixed firm, so the film inside was dry.

I had one more stop before I could board the train. I walked to the commandant's villa, my heart hammering against my ribs. The cobblestone streets of Oswiecim were deserted. Coils of black smoke filled the air, bricks littered the pavement, and doors hung smoldering on their hinges. I picked my way through the rubble to the commandant's house. I headed straight for the music room. I don't know what I was looking for or what I expected to find, but it wasn't there. The room was a mess. The curtains reeked of urine, and the walls were doused with wine. The piano stool lay on its side, its black leather seat slashed. Beside it, the piano sloped on three legs, its hammers and strings wrenched from its frame. I climbed the stairs to Karl's room. The last time I was in the house, we'd kissed. I didn't want the memory distorted by shattered glass and splintered wood, but I had to say good-bye. If I couldn't say good-bye to Karl in person, then I'd say it to his paintbrush and easel, to his music and the books that he loved.

Karl's room had been his refuge, the only room in the house without a picture of Hitler, a room filled with art, music, and beauty. I stopped at the door and saw the easel in pieces on the ground, books smeared with paint, a shredded map. I stepped into the room, careful not to tread on the punctured tubes of paint lying on the floor, their blues, reds, and yellows leaking out of them. Above Karl's bed, the words *Die Nazi* bled on the wall.

I fell onto the bed and buried my face in Karl's sheets. The smell of him was everywhere, in the blankets and the pillows and the pages of his books. I ran my hands along his bookcase and saw his sketchbook on the top shelf. I pulled it from the shelf and opened it to the last page. The delicate girl with the pale eyes Karl had drawn all those months ago had changed. There was a new strength to her lines, less shading, more depth. She wasn't cowering in the shadows so much as stepping out of them. I tore the sheet from the book and stuffed it into my pocket.

I sat down at the piano and ran my fingers along the paint-splattered keys. My fingers found a bloodred C-sharp, then an angry purple D. I hadn't played piano for a month, hadn't thought about Clara Schumann in weeks, but my fingers found the heartbreaking opening to her Romance in A Minor. I played the love song for my mother, tears streaming down my face. She'd been so thrilled when I'd told her I'd be playing piano with the Birkenau Women's Orchestra. I remembered her standing in front of the watchtower staring wide-eyed at the thin-armed players.

I bore down on the keys, and Clara's music filled the room.

"I promised to play Clara for you, Anyu," I shouted above the chords. "I promised never to give up."

Chapter 20

It felt strange sitting in a train with windows and leather seats and a door I could slide open. I found a window seat and spent the next ten days following the curve of the tracks that would take me home. The train emptied slowly: Poles, Russians, Ukrainians, Romanians, Hungarians, everyone heading home or heading out, scrambling to start a new life, searching for a new home.

As we neared Hungary, I lifted my eyes to the rolling green hills, the wide stretches of farmland, the grassy banks of the Danube. I saw goats and cows, oak and acacia, and for the first time, I dared to believe that I could leave the camp, really leave. I'd stopped looking over my shoulder and shoveling food into my mouth. I'd stopped scratching at imaginary fleas and standing at attention. My hair was long enough to comb and part on the side. I'd put on weight. People called me by my name; they asked if I was hungry. I mattered.

We zigzagged through Eger, Budapest, and Szolnok. At night I dreamed not of Karl or the camps, but of home. I was back in the bedroom I shared with Erika. She was brushing her hair; I was reading a book. I could smell challah baking, and the sweet, spicy mix of paprika and brown onion frying in a pan. It was Friday night, and Mother was shelling peas in the kitchen, waiting for Father to return from synagogue. I heard his key in the lock and his footsteps in the hallway, and I ran to greet him.

I leaped off the train as soon as the stationmaster opened the doors. I was in Debrecen — I was home. Except it didn't feel like home. The station looked the same, but no one was waiting for me on the platform. The cobblestone streets still tripped me up. There were ducks in the pond and skaters on the ice rink, ice-cream vendors outside the park and boats on the lake. It was as if nothing had changed — but everything had — and I felt like a stranger. I passed traders at their market stalls and children eating doughnuts outside the Piac Street bakery. No one smiled, and no one stopped me.

I hurried toward Hatvan Street, to the safe familiarity of the Jewish quarter, surprised to see it so unchanged. I stopped at the end of our street. I craned my neck and looked for our apartment building. It was still there, just before the bend, its whitewashed walls in need of paint. Flowers spilled from the balconies; washing hung on the rails. I pulled my C-sharp from my pocket and raced up the hill. The front door was open. I ran inside, climbed the stairs to the fifth floor, two at a time, and stopped at the door to our apartment. The mezuzah was missing and the welcome mat had been replaced, but the brass plate still read *Apartment 5B*. Vera had warned me not to get my hopes up, but I could smell fish frying, and when I pressed my ear to the door, I swear I heard a noise.

I swallowed hard and knocked on the door.

"Hello." A woman swung the door open. She was holding a wooden spoon and wearing an apron embroidered with strawberries. Her cheeks were dusted with flour. She was smiling until she saw me, then her smile slipped away.

"What do you want?" she asked, folding her arms across her chest and stepping in front of the door.

"This is my apartment. . . . I-I've been away," I stammered.

"Yes, and while you were away, *we* moved in." It wasn't an apology. "You're trespassing." She stepped toward me, forcing me back into the hallway. "And if you don't leave, I'll call the police."

My mouth fell open. Call the police? She was in my

home, leaving floury footprints on my hallway runner, switching on my lights and using my oven.

I elbowed her aside and ran down the corridor, past my father's umbrella stand and my mother's white orchid. I reached the bedroom I shared with Erika and lunged for the door. I needed to touch something that was Erika's, something from before.

"That's my daughter's room. Don't you dare." The woman caught up to me. Her eyes were cold, her mouth hard. She grabbed my arm and dragged me from the door.

"It's *my* room." I shook free of her grip. I imagined that behind the door, my room was just as I'd left it, the pictures of Puccini and Verdi still tacked to the wall. The dollhouse Father had built for my seventh birthday under the window, the clothes I'd sewn for my dolls in a shoe box under my bed. I pushed the door open and stepped into the room, horrified to find that the woman was right. It wasn't my room. There were no concert programs or ticket stubs taped to the mirror and no scuffed school shoes poking out from under the bed. Instead there were porcelain ponies on the windowsill, an unfinished tapestry on the bed, and a large brown bear tucked under the sheets. A photo of a girl I didn't know sat in a silver frame on top of the bedside table.

"Have a couple been here?" I turned on the woman. "They probably look like me—skinny, with short hair. They're in their forties. He might have a beard; she has blond hair. . . ." I paused to catch my breath. "And a girl a little older than me? Darker, with brown eyes. She's feisty. You'd remember her." I grabbed her blouse. "Her name is Erika. Please, you can have everything—"

"I already do." The woman pulled away. "Now get out." She snatched a cushion from the chair in the hallway and flung it at me. I stumbled out the door, clutching the cushion. The stitching had unraveled a little, but I could still make out my mother's careful letters: a blue *E* for *Erika,* a red *H* for *Hanna,* a heart beside the letter *E,* a black treble clef next to the *H.*

I staggered downstairs and into the back garden and stood on the silvered lawn, a knot of anger rising in my belly. The yard was dark. I was alone. There were no guards with guns, no dogs, no one to stop me from screaming. And still I clamped my hand over my mouth. If I started yelling, I might never stop, and if I didn't stop, if I let the anger leak out of me, what would be left? I hugged the cushion to my chest and pictured my mother bent over her sewing machine, pumping the foot pedal with her stockinged feet, a smile on her lips. If I gave voice to my anger, if I went back upstairs and beat down the door and took what was mine, I'd still be no closer to knowing what had become of my family. I kicked at the frozen ground. It was so unfair. I rammed the ground again. A clod of earth loosened under my boot. I dug the wet ball from the ground and threw it at the back wall, watching as the dirt and ice slid down the brickwork. I bent down and plunged my hands back into the wet soil. My fingernails were filthy with mud just like — I shot up and ran to the back of the apartment building, holding up five fingers. Papa had held up five fingers, then taken five steps to the right the night before the roundup, the night he'd buried our savings in the backyard. I took five steps to the right. How many steps after that? I closed my eyes and tried to recall the words Papa had mouthed, tried to picture him stepping into the garden clutching the battered cookie tin. Three. He'd taken three steps backward into the garden. I took three steps back and bent down to plunge my hands into the earth, but when I looked down at the ground, the soil had already been dug up.

Papa?

I turned and ran to my old school. I don't know why I ended up there, outside the music-room window. I guess I hoped Papa might be there, waiting for me.

He'd often stop by the music room. He liked to watch me play. I wiped an arc across the frosted windowpane and saw the violins, flutes, and cymbals stacked on their shelves; the trumpets on the floor, the trombones next to them, and in the middle of the room, my piano. I'd spent more time at that piano than in the lunchroom with my classmates.

I stumbled on until I reached the synagogue on Pásti Street. I wasn't looking for God, just somewhere to sleep for the night. Rabbi Myerson sat hunched on a wooden chair by the pulpit. His gray suit was creased and worn, his eyes dull. He looked up from his prayer book.

"Hannale, you're alive! When I came out of hiding..." He shook his head. "The synagogue's empty. I'd hoped there were others who had hidden, like me, others with brave neighbors." He paused. "Birkenau?"

I nodded.

"How did you escape the march?"

I didn't answer for a long time. I was thinking about Karl. He'd chosen me at the audition. He'd offered up the name of his fifth-grade geography teacher when I was caught playing Mendelssohn, and warned me about the infirmary. He'd lied to his father to keep me from being evacuated, and followed me into a snowstorm to keep me safe. He was the reason I was still here.

"A brave boy helped me."

"And your parents? Your sister?"

I shrugged. "I was hoping you would know."

The rabbi put his hand on mine. "You'll find a bed and a warm meal at the Jewish Community Center on Radnor Street, and a notice board on the first floor." He shifted in his seat. "If your parents are alive, their names will be on it." He looked down at the yellowing pages of Hebrew script. "I pray they were spared. They were good people."

The community center on Radnor Street had been converted into a home for refugees. It was a shelter for those who had been turned away from their homes. I found the notice board the rabbi had spoken of. I ran my finger down the list of survivors until I reached the letter *M*. There was only one name under Mendel: *Hanna Mendel, discharged from Auschwitz, 14th February, 1945*. I sank to the floor.

"Just because their names aren't there doesn't mean they didn't survive."

I looked up at the sound of a familiar voice. A young man with a thin face and a thick red beard hovered over me.

"Not all the camps have been emptied. I'm waiting for my mother. We were separated in Auschwitz." He looked down at me. "You don't recognize me, do you?"

I shook my head.

"It's me, Michael Wollner." He held out his hand and helped me to my feet.

"You've changed," I said.

We all had.

Michael showed me where to collect my blanket and bowl and how to register for my weekly allowance of 22 pengö. We sat in the school hall, ate dinner together, and talked until they turned the lights out. We talked about Auschwitz and our lives before the war and what we planned to do next. He had so many plans. Mostly he wanted to start over. He'd heard of Jews being smuggled into Palestine. He planned to join them and help build the Jewish state. He was learning to fight. He was training to get strong.

"Dachau, Bergen-Belsen — there are dozens of camps the Russians haven't reached. When they do, that list downstairs will run to ten pages. Maybe our parents' names will be on it."

I hoped he was right.

"You're not the boy I remember from school." A moment passed before he answered.

"I guess I've grown up. You're exactly the same as I remember."

He smiled and I smiled back. It felt good to be Hanna Mendel from before the war. A girl who had parents. A girl who had plans. A girl with a scholarship. I wanted to be that girl again. Maybe with Michael I could be. My smile wasn't as wide as his, but it was a start and it felt good. It was easy with Michael, uncomplicated. We were both caught halfway between the past and the future. I didn't tell him about Karl.

We agreed to meet up again in the morning. Michael went upstairs to the men's wing, but I couldn't sleep. I wandered the corridors, looking for a music room, somewhere I could find myself and lose myself at the same time. I found a door on the third floor marked ORCHESTRA. I pushed it open, fumbled around for a switch, and turned on the light. The instruments had all been packed away, but in the center of the room was a shiny black piano. Butted up against it was a mattress. And curled up on the mattress, like a question mark, was my sister.

"Erika! Erika, it's me!" I shook her awake.

She blinked at the light, then she blinked at me.

"Hanna!" she shrieked as she leaped from her bed. "Hanna!" she cried, and she wrapped me in her arms.

"Hanna!" she whispered, and tears rolled down her cheeks.

We clung to each other like limpets, repeating each other's names, stroking each other's hair, kissing each other's cheeks. I didn't tire of hearing her say my name. I planted a kiss on her nose. She was alive. My sister was alive. I grabbed Erika's hands and spun her around, once, twice, three times, till we were both dizzy with happiness.

Erika pulled me onto the mattress. "When you didn't see my name on the list of survivors, you must've thought I was dead. My name's not there because I wasn't liberated from a camp," she said. "I escaped. I made it to Debrecen very late last night, found this place, and snuck up here, and when I saw the music room, well, it seemed like the perfect place to wait for you."

"You escaped?"

Erika's smile disappeared. "You waved me good-bye at the main gate, remember? It was snowing. We'd been told we were going to work in a factory. I knew they were lying. I wanted to say good-bye. I wanted to tell you I wasn't coming back, but I knew you'd come with me or make a scene, and I couldn't let that happen." Erika shook her head. "We walked for hours. People collapsed in the snow. The guards shot anyone who couldn't keep up. I was so tired and cold, but I kept going. I had to keep going—I knew you'd be waiting for me."

"And you did. . . ." I kissed her cheek.

"But if Piri hadn't been there . . ."

"Piri?" I stared at her.

"Piri was on the same march. She dragged me through the snow. I never would've made it without her." She stood up and walked to the window. She looked shrunken, diluted. "We walked for two days, maybe more. A Polish prisoner told us we were headed for a train station. Piri said we weren't getting on any train. She knew I wouldn't survive another day without food, so she came up with a plan. The next time someone stumbled and the guards took aim, we'd collapse and pretend we were dead."

"The guards could've shot you." My stomach clenched.

"It was a chance we had to take."

I rose from the bed and walked to the window. I held Erika's small hands in mine and waited for her to continue.

"At the next round of gunfire, we both fell to the snow. The prisoners marched past. When we finally raised our heads, there were no prisoners or guards, just a few Polish peasants with a cart. They were collecting bodies, clearing them from the road for the SS. When they went to pull Piri from the roadside, she told them the Red Army was closing in and that if they spared us, we'd speak well of them if they were charged as collaborators."

"So the plan worked?"

Erika nodded. "They helped us onto the cart and drove us to their farm. They let us sleep in the stable and share the scraps they fed their pigs. We hid there till the Russians arrived. Then I came looking for you."

"And Piri?" I held my breath. I imagined my teacher renting an apartment near the Karlsplatz and playing piano with the Vienna Philharmonic, or living near the Parc de la Villette and teaching piano at the Paris Conservatory.

"She's headed for Italy and, from there, to Australia."

"Australia?"

Erika nodded. "It's as far away from Europe as you can get." She turned toward me, her eyebrows raised. "We could join her. Or we could go somewhere else. New York. London. We can start again. I'll go to university; you can play piano."

I shook my head.

"Erika, we'll need to get jobs. The money Papa left us . . . I dug up the ground. It's . . ."

Erika's face split into a smile. She lifted the mattress from the floor.

"Here?"

Under the mattress was Father's cookie tin. Erika tossed it to me. I pried open the lid and pulled out father's pocket watch — 11:46 p.m. It was still keeping time.

"Paris and New York sound wonderful." I wrapped my arms around my sister's narrow waist. "But we're not going anywhere. Not till we've heard about Anyu and Papa."

Chapter 21

I dragged a mattress into the music room, and we set up a makeshift home. We slept together, between the piano and the wind instruments. We ate in the hall and showered on the third floor, in the women's gymnasium. I wanted to return to Hatvan Street and demand our apartment back, but Erika was against it. The military police wouldn't help us, and Erika had heard of too many Jews being chased from their homes. When Mr. Faranc, our neighbor, forced his way back into apartment 12A, I begged Erika to reconsider. But when Mr. Faranc's body was found floating facedown in Lake Bekas two days later, I dropped the subject.

The days snaked past slowly. Daylight lengthened, melting the last of the snow. We agreed not to mourn for our parents, not till we knew. We looked for their names on the first-floor notice board every morning before breakfast and every evening before bed. We looked for them at the synagogue and at the doughnut shop in Hatvan Street. We put up posters at the train station. We celebrated Passover in March at the Community Center and left two empty chairs at the Seder table, just in case. We set aside a bowl of chicken soup for Anyu and saved a slice of gefilte fish for Papa, but we celebrated the end of slavery under Pharoah — and our own liberation — alone.

I told Erika about Karl and our last days together. I didn't tell her that remembering him hurt, or that I thought of him almost as often as I thought of Anyu and Papa.

"Karl did the right thing," Erika told me, "and so have you. You had to let him go, for both your sakes."

I tried to let him go. I tried to fill the emptiness with music. I practiced piano every day. I played every composer Hitler banned and every piece of music the commandant detested. I practiced till my fingers hurt. With my weekly allowance from the relief fund, I didn't have to work, so I filled my days reading books and hiking in the hills. I did all the things I'd dreamed of doing in the camp. I picnicked in the park with friends. I went to the circus, and I taught myself to ride a bike. I went to my first wedding.

There were so many weddings in Debrecen, so many people looking to replace lost loves and lost children. I wasn't looking to replace a lost love. I was looking for the old Hanna Mendel, the girl I used to be—the woman I was meant to become. So I let Michael trail after me as I wandered Debrecen's roadways, and I let him accompany me to the park when I fed the ducks. I let him sit in the music room and watch me practice. It felt good being with someone who understood how I ached. It felt good being among my own people. After everything that had happened, I was still a Jew. Not because I'd been locked in a cattle train or branded with a tattoo. Baking challah with my mother, lighting the Sabbath candles, eating latkes on Hanukkah—that's what being a Jew meant.

I couldn't run from it. And I didn't want to.

The number of concentration camp survivors grew, but my parents' names didn't appear on the list. In April, three camps in Germany—Buchenwald, Bergen-Belsen, and Dachau—were liberated, and the list on the first-floor pin-board ran to six sheets. On the eighth of May 1945, Germany surrendered and the war was over. On the tenth of May, the printed list of survivors was taken down.

Erika and I sat shiva that day. We mourned for our parents as Jewish custom demanded. We tore our clothes and sat on low stools and prayed to God to protect their souls. I didn't play the piano. We didn't go out. We clung to each other and the memories we shared: Father at his workbench, smiling over his spectacles; Mother in the kitchen, humming to Bartok as she baked. We didn't have photos to pore over. I couldn't run to my mother's dresser and inhale her perfume or fling Father's drawers open and find a scarf to put on. There were no mementos of their life with which we could comfort ourselves, no bits left behind, so we told each other stories and helped each other remember.

We hid in our cocoon, but we had to emerge eventually. After seven days of mourning, we bathed and dressed. We lit a memorial candle and placed it on top of the piano beside Papa's pocket watch. I played Liszt's Hungarian Rhapsody for my mother, and Erika sang my father's favorite Yiddish lullaby, the same one he'd sung to us every night when we were young. We kept the pocket watch to remember Father, and Mother's wedding band to remember her, and buried the skullcap and prayer book by the lake in the Puszta forest.

I stood over the sad mound of dirt and tried not to cry.

"A gold watch and a wedding band," I said. "That's all we have left of them." I looked at Erika. "Papa would have wanted a Jewish burial, like Opapa's."

"They were kept behind a brick wall in the ghetto and then locked in a barrack. I wouldn't want them in a box in the ground," Erika said.

I looked up at the sky and tried to imagine my parents hovering somewhere above the hunger and pain, stretching their legs and fanning out their arms on their way to the next life.

"They're free," I said.

Erika nodded.

I found a smooth, gray stone and placed it on the mound of dirt—a piece of Debrecen, a rock to last for all time.

"We'll never forget you," I whispered. "We'll live the lives you wanted us to live. We'll make you proud."

When Michael asked me to accompany him to a moonlight concert three days later, I said yes, because my parents had always liked Michael and because it made sense. We'd lived through the same experience and been on the same side. I knew it was a date. I'd promised to live the life my parents wanted me to live, so I agreed.

"I'll meet you at the park at six," Michael said, his grin as wide as the Balaton River.

"It's a date," I said, trying to mirror his mood.

And then he looked me in the eye and said, "I

know you've always dreamed of performing in Paris, and I'd never stop you from chasing your dreams." His stare unglued me. "They have an orchestra in Palestine, a fully equipped symphony orchestra." His cheeks turned apple-red. "And an opera company and a broadcasting station."

I forced myself to concentrate. The mere mention of the word *opera* had me back at the villa, daydreaming of Karl. He was standing over me, singing *Tristan and Isolde*. We were alone. He was stroking the back of my neck. . . .

"You wouldn't be the first concert pianist to settle in Palestine. Weissenberg is there; Kestenberg, too."

I escaped to the music room when he paused for breath. Erika found me in front of a mirror, putting on lipstick.

"You can't paint your smile on," she said, taking the lipstick and sitting down. I sat down next to her. "You know Michael's mad about you."

I nodded.

"Is that what you want?"

"What I want?" I said, getting to my feet. I wanted to stop thinking about Karl. I wanted my old life back. I wanted to want Michael Wollner. "I want Anyu and Papa back." *I want Karl to walk through that door.* I grabbed my jacket from a peg on the door and my bag from the bed. "It doesn't matter what *I* want. Michael's a decent person, Erika. A nice person. A Jew. I promised Anyu and Papa I'd do the right thing. . . ."

"You're right," Erika said, stepping in front of me. "You owe it to Anyu and Papa to do the right thing — to be happy. Don't give in to fear now."

I walked past Erika and swung the door open. It was ten minutes to six.

It was a short walk to the park. I arrived early and sat down on a bench. Michael would be here in five minutes. *Michael. I was choosing Michael.* I looked down at my watch and stared at the minute hand, inching slowly toward the twelve. In four minutes, my future would begin. I took a deep breath, stood up, and grabbed my bag.

Chapter 22

I fed a sheet of paper into the typewriter. Mrs. Hermann closed the door to the office, whispering "Good luck" as she left. Her workday at the community center was done, and I could have the room until the next day. I reached into my bag, pulled out Karl's scarf, and slipped it around my neck. Erika was right. My parents wanted me to be happy. My mother had told me never to give up. Choosing Michael would be a betrayal. I'd promised Anyu and Papa to do whatever it took to make it out of the camp, and I had. I'd promised to live a full and happy life, and keep playing piano, and I would. I'd promised to tell the world what Hitler had done.

I addressed my letter to General Kafelnikov, First Army of the Ukrainian Front, Birkenau, Poland. *You have a prisoner,* I typed. *His name is Karl Jager and he saved my life.*

I pulled my C-sharp from my pocket and felt the familiar soft grain under my fingers. I laid it down on the desk and returned to the keys. I started at the beginning, in the Debrecen ghetto, with a guard banging at my door. I wrote about my father handing over the keys to our apartment, and the rats at the Serly brickyards. I wrote about the dark, damp cattle train and my father's wet, stubbled cheeks. I wrote about Mengele's steel baton, and the chimneys belching smoke. I wrote about the razor blades and tattoos and our burned scalps and blistered hands. I wrote about the stale bread and black water, and playing piano on my mother's back. I wrote about Erika and the twins.

It was almost midnight by the time I typed the commandant's name. The pages filled with black ink and floated to the floor. I was hungry and tired, but the general had to know what the commandant had done to Stanislaw, what he would've done to me if I'd played the wrong note. Mostly, I wrote about Karl. The general didn't know Karl had called us by our names or smuggled food into Birkenau. He didn't know that when the commandant was away, Karl brought me food. He didn't know that he had the wrong boy.

The morning light filtered through the office shutters. I reached into my bag and took Erika's film from its hiding place. I slid the typed sheets and the film into an envelope and addressed it to the general. I'd kept my promise to my father to tell the world what I'd seen. I hoped I'd done enough to secure Karl's release.

I imagined him in the POW camp, alone and scared.

I fed another sheet of paper into the typewriter.

Dear Karl,

The black and white keys thrummed when I struck them. There was so much I wanted to say, I didn't know where to begin.

I'm in Debrecen with Erika.

I stared at the keys, worrying over what to write next, wondering what Clara Wieck would have written to Robert Schumann.

I never told you the end of Clara and Robert's story. They were separated for three years. They reunited in Paris and married against her father's wishes.

I pulled an envelope from the drawer and put it on the desk, next to my C-sharp.

They can't keep you forever. I'll wait.

I addressed the envelope to Karl, scooped up the C-sharp, and looked down at my hand. The note gleamed against my pale skin, blistered and splintering at the edges but still whole. I slipped it into the envelope.

I want you to have my C-sharp. You can return it when we see each other.

Until then,

Hanna

Author's Note

Playing for the Commandant is a work of historical fiction. The characters in the novel are created from my imagination, but the Debrecen ghetto and the Serly brickyards; the cattle trains packed with innocent men, women, and children; and the Auschwitz-Birkenau concentration camp, where they were brought to die in the summer of 1944, existed. Dr. Mengele stood on the ramp and sent the startled people who stood before him to the right or to the left, to the labor force or to the gas chambers. There was a commandant of Birkenau, every bit as cruel and sadistic as Commandant Jager, and an orchestra that was forced to play marches at the camp's main gate.

Six million Jews were murdered during the Holocaust, over one million of them at the Birkenau death camp in Poland. The Nazis believed that Jews were racially inferior and a threat to their community. They also targeted the Roma people and the disabled, as well as those they considered political, ideological, or behavioral threats, such as communists, socialists, Jehovah's Witnesses, and homosexuals. Of the 1.1 million Jews murdered at Birkenau, nearly half were Hungarian.

I learned about the Holocaust from my father, who was thirteen years old when he was loaded onto a cattle train bound for Auschwitz. My father didn't tell me his story until I was an adult and he was diagnosed with a terminal illness. He was given six months to live, so we were running out of time. He hadn't told me about his Holocaust experience earlier because he thought that the best way to move past the horror and build a new life in Australia was to put it behind him. I knew that the only way to ensure that it wouldn't happen again was to keep talking about it.

And writing about it. So I wrote his story down. I started reading other stories and watching movies about the Holocaust and reading history books. Then I wrote this book. I don't pretend to know how it felt to be imprisoned in Birkenau. I don't think anyone who wasn't there can ever really understand. But it's important to try. Reading history books and memoirs, talking about the Holocaust and writing about it are the best ways to stop it from happening again.

Acknowledgments

My heartfelt thanks to my friends and classmates in the professional writing and editing course at RMIT for their intelligence, support, and advice. To Clare Renner for her encouragement and Olga Lorenzo for her honesty. To my writing group—Brooke Maggs, Richard Holt, Carla Fedi, and Deryn Mansell—for their enthusiasm and their time, and to Ilka Tampke, especially, for inspiring me with her writing and never tiring of mine.

Thanks to Andrew Kelly for believing in this story, to Maryann Ballantyne for her sensitivity and intelligence in helping me shape it, to Mary Verney for her brilliant copyedit, and Suzanne O'Sullivan for her excellent proofreading.

Thanks also to Sue Hampel for allowing me to raid her library and to Dr. Bill Anderson for his expert advice, guidance, and generosity.

And finally, to my husband, Shaun, and our three beautiful children, Josh, Tanya, and Remy, for loving me.